The Comstock Camels

The
Comstock
Camels

Gary McCarthy

A DOUBLE D WESTERN
DOUBLEDAY
New York London Toronto Sydney Auckland

A DOUBLE D WESTERN
PUBLISHED BY DOUBLEDAY
a division of Bantam Doubleday Dell Publishing Group, Inc.
666 Fifth Avenue, New York, New York 10103

Double D Western, Doubleday,
and the portrayal of the letters DD
are trademarks of Doubleday, a division of
Bantam Doubleday Dell Publishing Group, Inc.

Library of Congress Cataloging-in-Publication Data

McCarthy, Gary.
The Comstock camels/Gary McCarthy.—1st ed.
    p. cm.—(Double D western)
I. Title.
PS3563.C3373C65   1993
813'.54—dc20   92-31938
CIP

ISBN 0-385-41990-2
Copyright © 1993 by Gary McCarthy
All Rights Reserved
Printed in the United States of America
April 1993
First Edition

10 9 8 7 6 5 4 3 2 1

For Dr. Dave Ganzel—
longtime friend, veterinarian
and animal lover
(even camels)

The Comstock Camels

One

THE DERBY MAN balanced a thick stack of hand-written manuscript pages on his lap. An expensive Cuban cigar protruded from his lips and his black eyes shone with delight as he glanced up from the manuscript toward Miss Dolly Beavers, who had her hands full maneuvering their carriage up a very steep, winding Sierra road.

"Dolly, my love, this latest manuscript, *The Glory Guns*, may well become my finest dime novel yet! It has all the elements my readers have come to expect—excitement, color, blood and bullets."

Dolly risked a sideways glance at the man she adored. Darby Buckingham looked so elegant and refined with his black suit and derby, starched white shirt and silk tie. Oh sure, he was slightly past his prime, but Darby was *so* strong and masculine. A real gentleman, rich and famous, who had promised to marry her.

"Read me the ending, please?"

"You know that I'm a little superstitious about reading my work before its final revisions."

"I know, but *please!*"

"Oh," Darby relented, powerless to refuse this woman. "All right."

Darby chewed his cigar for a moment as he located the conclusion of this latest Buckingham novel. He cleared his throat and began to read, "Though badly wounded, Durango stood his ground and kept pulling the triggers of his pearl-handled sixguns. Blazing guns dealing double doses of lead

poisoning. And when his guns were empty and two desperadoes yet remained standing, Durango yanked a Bowie knife
from his boot and snarled, 'If yer real men, let's play with
steel and dance with death!'

"The last two desperadoes gulped. Quaking with terror,
they collapsed to their knees and begged for their miserable
lives.

"Durango's thin lips twisted with utter contempt, then he
spun on his bootheel and limped into the fiery sunset, his
silhouette edged with gold and the blade of his Bowie glittering like polished silver."

Darby stopped reading. His eyes grew misty and he could
see Durango limping off into the sunset. Darby had difficulty
speaking because the image of his latest western hero was so
powerful in his fertile mind. "Well, Dolly, how do you like
the ending of *The Glory Guns?*"

Dolly's ample bosom swelled with pride and she also
choked with pride and emotion. "It's . . . it's a master-
piece!"

"Really?"

"Oh yes, my darling! It's prose for the ages! When will you
stop this torture and let me read the entire manuscript?"

"When we reach Lake Tahoe," Darby Buckingham promised, his ink pen scratching in last-minute changes. "You
know how superstitious I am about my work before I make
my final revisions."

"I know," Dolly said as she expertly negotiated their rented
team of horses around another hairpin curve on the steep
narrow road. "You are *such* a perfectionist. But sometimes, my
darling, I can hardly stand the suspense."

The carriage bounced over a rock and Darby's pen skidded
wetly across the page. "Oh blast!" he swore. "Now look what
I've done!"

"Why don't you just put the manuscript away, sweetheart?
After all, we will have plenty of time to make those itty bitty
changes while we vacation all summer long beside the lake."

"Vacation? Ha!" Darby barked, patting the letter he had

received from Zack and Bear, their crazy old mountain man friends. "Have you forgotten the contents of their message?"

"No, but . . ."

"They need help. Oh sure, they paid some scribe a few dollars to make it sound as if everything was rosy, but if you'd read between the lines as I did, you'd know that their latest venture is failing."

Dolly frowned. "I can't for the life of me understand why they'd buy a steamboat! Neither one of them knows the first thing about engines or boats."

"Beats me too," Darby admitted. "Some shyster probably sold them on the idea that they could get rich quick ferrying logs across the lake from one lumber mill to another."

"They'll never change," Dolly said, reaching over to pat Darby's knee. "And I'm sure they do need help, but that doesn't mean we can't also enjoy a cool summer in these lovely pines. Maybe even rent a boat that you can row around the shoreline so I can feed all the sweet ducks."

Darby did not find that prospect at all enticing. Lake Tahoe probably had seventy miles of shoreline and he wasn't about to row anyone around its perimeter. Besides, it was obvious that Dolly didn't know that the lake could get very rough during sudden and frequent afternoon squalls.

Still, he supposed he ought to be a little more jovial at the prospect of spending time in this mountain paradise with such a beautiful woman. Even now he could hardly keep from admiring the way the sun turned Dolly's blond locks to a rich gold and her cheeks to an apple's shine.

He forced his attention back to his manuscript but a moment later Darby swore as the carriage bounced over another rock and his pen skidded again across the page.

"Please, darling, put the manuscript away until we are settled in at the lake," Dolly said. "I know you are very excited about it, but the best things are worth waiting for."

Darby looked over at her very quickly but Dolly's eyes were glued to the backs of their carriage horses. He did notice, however, that there was a smug smile tugging at the corners

of her mouth and he knew she was delighted with her own
flash of rare philosophical insight.

The Derby Man took a deep breath of the pure mountain
air. The scent of pines and sage was invigorating. To his left
spread the entire Carson Valley including the flourishing
ranch community of Genoa, the oldest settlement in Nevada.
It had been founded by the Mormons and they had been
extremely upset when Brigham Young had ordered them back
to Utah leaving their land and hard-earned improvements.
The story was that the Mormons, angered because they could
not get fair offers for their prosperous Genoa farms and
ranches, had cursed their valley with fire, flood and winds. At
least the wind part had come true. It picked up strong almost
every afternoon.

"I hope Bear and Zack have a cozy cabin ready for us,"
Dolly said. "I'm not going to be satisfied sleeping all summer
in a tent."

"We'll find a cabin," Darby vowed, his eyes returning to
the manuscript in his lap.

Dolly saw that he was again preoccupied by his manuscript.
"I wish you'd put it away and pay more attention to me and
our lovely surroundings."

"I will," he promised. "Just a few more changes while my
creative juices are bubbling. This scene where Durango is
bound hand and foot, then thrown into a rattlesnake-infested
pit might be a little too sensational. Here, let me read it to
you so that you can give me your opinion."

"But I love *everything* you write, dear."

"I know, but it would help sometimes if you at least told me
which scenes you love more than others."

"I'll try—but it won't be easy."

"Thank you," Darby said. "Now, in this case, I . . ."

Darby's next words were forgotten as their carriage horses
suddenly stopped, braced their legs far apart and began to
snort with fear. Both animals had been perfectly well behaved
since being rented in Carson City but they now acted as if
they were about to lose their minds.

"Easy," Dolly yelped, tightening her lines as the horses began to dance and whirl about. "Darby, help!"

"What the deuce is the matter with them!" Darby shouted. He took the lines and struggled to control the animals as errant pages of *The Glory Guns* spilled across his feet. "They're acting as if they were being attacked by a swarm of hornets!"

"Don't let them turn or we'll tip over the mountainside and roll all the way to the bottom of this canyon!" Dolly exclaimed, hanging on for her life.

Darby was not an accomplished reinsman any more than he was adept with a rope or a sixgun. But being a former circus strong man and a bare knuckles fighter, he was enormously powerful and not one to be easily intimidated by man or beast. However, it was all he could do to keep the crazed horses from spinning around and sending their carriage over the edge.

"Whoa!" he bellowed. "Dammit, whoa!"

But Darby's efforts had no effect on the team and they continued to try to reverse direction on the precipitous mountain road.

"Here," Darby yelled, shoving the lines to Dolly. "I'm going to grab their bits!"

Dolly took the lines as Darby jumped from the carriage, oblivious to the fact that a cloud of manuscript papers followed in his wake. The fool horses were rolling their eyes, shaking their heads and acting as if they'd gone mad.

"What in the devil has gotten into you," Darby demanded, grabbing the bridles of both fractious horses.

"Darby! Look! Oh no!"

The Derby Man twisted around and blinked in astonishment to see a huge camel. The camel bared its long yellow teeth, hissed, squawked and spit a cupful of greenish goo that struck Darby in the chest. Before Darby could react, many more camels loomed into view, all of them squawking and spitting at him. It was all too much for Darby and the team of horses, whose last thread of reason snapped. They spun away in terror, and Darby, hands still locked into their bridles, was catapulted skyward. A shout of warning filled his throat as the crazed horses flew off the mountainside. Darby heard Dolly scream as he fell. The scream ended very painfully when he struck a rock, ripped out a clump of brush and went bouncing end over end down the mountainside. Halfway down, he flattened a small pine tree and that was all that he remembered until he and the carriage plunged into the icy river far below.

The shock of icy water made the Derby Man's body contract. He was not a young man but his fighter's instincts brought him storming to his feet as if roused by a bell.

Standing chest deep in the rushing river, he batted water from his eyes and pivoted around, losing his balance and tumbling over and over in the powerful current.

"Dolly!" he shouted, righting himself and looking frantically up and down the rapids. "Dolly!"

He didn't see her. His cries echoed up and down in the narrow canyon, banging off the granite walls as they funneled down to the Carson Valley.

"Dolly!"

Darby fought down his own rising panic. The carriage was collapsed on its roof, only the bottom half of its four wheels breaking the river's boiling surface. One of the horses was dead and floating half submerged in its traces, neck twisted at a sharp angle. The other horse was nowhere in sight.

"Dolly!" he shouted, as he bucked the swift current. "Dolly!"

Darby threw himself at the carriage, grabbed it and reached under where the seat would be, groping for the woman. In a mixture of relief and horror, his fingers tangled in Dolly's long blond hair.

"Oh blast!" he cried. Then he ducked under the water to try to pull the trapped woman free.

But despite his best efforts, Dolly was pinned and the current was making things even more difficult by pushing the overturned carriage down even harder. With a roar of anger, Darby surged up from the current. He took several deep breaths and his massive biceps knotted like the branches of an oak tree. His thick neck seemed to melt into his muscle-humped shoulders. Then he inhaled deeply and shot back under the carriage.

The water was alive. It pressed the carriage hard against Darby's shoulders as he wedged them under the seat cushion. Planting his round-toed shoes solidly on the riverbed, Darby heaved upward with all of his might. The carriage quivered. Its weight, coupled with the mass of the dead horse entangled in harness, was a mighty anchor, and yet . . . so great was the Derby Man's determination and strength that the entire affair slowly broke free of its rocky moorings.

Darby could feel the blood pounding in his ears as the current tried to bowl him over. His thick legs trembled with exertion until his knees finally locked and his head broke the water's surface. He gulped in great lungfuls of air. The carriage teetered precariously on his broad shoulders and he made a desperate stab toward Dolly, who appeared blue and unconscious. The tips of his stubby fingers entwined in her hair and he yanked hard. Her body floated free of the carriage. It was shrouded in soggy manuscript pages and then the powerful current swept her downriver and out of his tenuous grasp.

Gathering every ounce of strength he yet possessed, Darby heaved the carriage away and threw himself over backward. The current spun him downriver and when Darby's vision cleared, he saw that Dolly was floating face down.

A groan escaped his lips and the Derby Man swam like a man possessed. A moment later, he grabbed Dolly by the arms and somehow managed to pull her up onto the shore. Darby rolled the unconscious woman onto her stomach and straddled her back. He grabbed her shoulders and pulled them back and forth, trying to clear Dolly's lungs of water. Every few seconds, he pounded the unconscious woman between the shoulder blades.

"Come on!" he cried in helpless fury. "Wake up!"

An eternity passed as Darby worked frantically to revive his

love. Dolly finally choked, then expelled cupfuls of river water. The sound of her awful retching was music to Darby
Buckingham's ears. When Dolly began to struggle, he rolled
her over onto her back and gazed into her bluish face. Dolly
was bruised and her long blond locks were fouled with moss,
sand and sticks, but she was still beautiful in his eyes.

"Darby?" she gasped, clinging to him as if he might be a
dream.

"Yes," he whispered, cradling her head in his lap. "It's all
right. Everything is all right now."

"What . . . what happened?"

Before he could answer, they both heard the distant, taunt-
ing squawk of the camel caravan shuffling its way down toward the Carson Valley.

"Damn those miserable, stinking beasts!" Darby howled.

"What are they doing here of all places?"

"Who knows," Darby said bitterly. "All I do know is that
the United States Army imported the wretched creatures into
the Southwest a few years before the Civil War. They were
supposed to be the answer to supplying the desert forts
mainly in New Mexico, Arizona and Nevada."

"I take it the experiment was not a success," Dolly said.

"There were a few successes but far more failures. In the
end, the entire experiment was judged a disaster because the
camels were far more trouble than they were worth. Somewhat sheepishly, the Army finally auctioned them off for a
pittance. Apparently, we had the extreme misfortune of meeting a few of those original army camels under the worst possible circumstances."

"Yes, and apparently they terrify domesticated American
livestock."

"So it would seem," Darby grumbled. "So it would seem."

Darby gazed up at the road high above them. Their fall had
been long and very, very steep. It was a miracle they were
alive.

Trying to booster his own devastated spirits, Darby said,
"We'll escape these high canyon walls, don't worry, my dear."

"With you, I never worry," she bravely answered.

Darby's chest swelled at such a fine compliment and he was about to say something else encouraging when he heard a loud, crashing noise in the brush.

"What's that!" Dolly cried with alarm. "A grizzly? Maybe a cougar!"

Darby snatched up a rock and jumped to his feet. "If it is, he's going to get beaned!"

"Oh look!" Dolly exclaimed. "It's one of our poor horses!"

Darby dropped the rock, feeling a little embarrassed. The horse was limping and bleeding from numerous wounds but when it saw them, it raised its head and whinnied hopefully.

"Get out of here, you fool!" Darby raged.

"No!" Dolly cried. "We've got to help the poor thing."

"That 'poor thing,' as you call it, is half the reason we are in this mess," Darby reminded her with exasperation. "If that horse and its partner hadn't pulled over the cliff, we'd be safe at Lake Tahoe by now."

"Where *is* its friend?"

The other horse had broken free of its traces and its body had been washed down the river only a few minutes after Darby had managed to revive Dolly.

"I'm afraid it is dead."

Tears sprang to Dolly's eyes. "How awful!"

Darby patted her sympathetically, aware of how much Dolly loved all animals. Even ones like this dumb horse who had nearly cost them their lives.

"We're all going to be just fine now," Darby said reassuringly, even as he again craned his head back to study their path down into this canyon. The mountainside was impossibly steep and composed of loose and treacherous shale. It would, Darby decided, bury even a mountain goat.

"We'll find a trail out," he said more to himself than to Dolly. "There *has* to be a game trail or something. If not, we'll follow this river down to the Carson Valley."

Dolly stared trance-like at the half-submerged wagon

wheels jutting out from the river. Suddenly she cried, "What happened to *The Glory Guns!*"

"Gone." Darby choked with a sudden rush of bitterness.

"Oh no, darling!"

"Yes, gone," he repeated. "There might be a few pages scattered up on the road above, but only a few."

"But . . . but can't you rewrite it? I'll bet . . ."

Darby shook his head emphatically. "It would never work. Instead of creating, I'd just be trying to remember inspired passages. Fragmentary descriptions would come hauntingly to mind, but they'd be mere bits and pieces serving only to torment me with the reminder of this devastating loss."

"Oh, Darby, are you sure?"

"Absolutely sure," he told her. "It would be like trying to breathe life back into something beautiful that had died. I may . . . I may never write again."

Dolly paled. "Don't say that!"

"It's true. This kind of catastrophe can devastate a writer's creative genius."

"But . . ."

Darby silenced her protest with a kiss. "Please," he said a moment later, "let's not think about *The Glory Guns* anymore."

"But what about your publisher! And all your readers! Darby, they've been waiting for months to read your next dime novel!"

"They'll survive," he told her. "Just as we will."

Darby went over to the horse. He knew nothing about horses, really, except that he did not like them. However, it seemed appropriate to do something, so he stroked the animal's bloody shoulder, then inspected its injured leg. Finally, he picked up the horse's foot and discovered a large rock wedged into the crevasses of its frog.

With a pen knife that he used to clip the ends off his Cuban cigars, Darby removed the rock.

"There," he said. "Try it now."

The horse obliged him by walking off a little ways. It was no longer limping.

"Darby," Dolly said, her voice thick with praise, "you keep saying you hate horses, but you really have a gifted way with them."

He blushed, then gazed down the river canyon, his mind still unable to shake the loss of his manuscript. Dolly was right. His publisher would be extremely upset and disappointed, as would his legions of readers. It had been six months since the Derby Man's latest dime novel had been published and everyone was getting impatient. They seemed to believe that Darby Buckingham alone could write the kind of exciting western dime novel that they craved.

A hawk sailed down through the canyon and caught Darby's eye. He watched the magnificent bird soar on the hot thermal winds sweeping up from the valley below to rise against these rugged slopes of the eastern Sierra Nevadas.

"Stop wallowing in self-pity about the manuscript," Darby roughly reminded himself in a low voice. "Think about getting Dolly to safety!"

Darby squared his broad shoulders. Somehow, he had to get himself, Dolly and the fool horse out of this deep, brush-clogged canyon. But even with that accomplished, Darby very much doubted if he would ever again be able to write his epic tales of western adventure.

Try as he might, Darby Buckingham had a sick feeling deep in his soul that he would always be a man haunted by the tragic loss of perhaps the finest but most ill-fated dime novel ever written, *The Glory Guns.*

Two

DARBY RETURNED to the horse, which had come to stand close by the river, head down, looking very repentant. At Darby's approach, it nickered hopefully, lower lip flapping with as much excitement as it could muster.

"It's all your fault," he said to the sorry animal. "If I had a gun—and if Dolly wasn't here—I'd seriously consider terminating your miserable life."

In reply, the bay gelding nudged Darby with its soft muzzle. Its huge brown eyes pleaded for mercy.

"All right," Darby said. "Dolly has a twisted knee, you look like you've been trampled by a herd of buffalo and I've lost the best manuscript I've ever written. So we're all in lousy shape. The thing we have to do now is to escape this canyon before the sun goes down."

The gelding nuzzled him again. Darby took pity on the beast and relieved it of most of its torn harness, which he then used to fashion a bridle and a lead line. He went over to Dolly and picked her up as easily as if she were a small child. Setting her on the horse, Darby said, "You hang on tight while I lead off to find a trail out of this canyon."

"Do you know what I was thinking?" Dolly asked, wrapping her fingers into the gelding's mane.

"What?"

"I recalled that we didn't see anyone leading or tending those awful camels. Wouldn't you think that *someone* would be present and be responsible for their despicable behavior?"

"I would," Darby said, leading the horse off downriver as

his eyes searched for an escape route. He spotted his battered derby floating in the shallows of the river and tied the horse up, then went to retrieve it. The derby was a sodden mess but he fisted it back into a rough semblance of its former shape. It still looked ridiculous with its bent, sagging brim but Darby yanked it down to his ears anyhow.

"That looks better already," Dolly said, as always trying to look at the brighter side of things.

"It looks stupid but it shades my eyes from the sun and keeps the tops of my ears from getting sunburned," Darby replied.

"Well," Dolly said, "at least I'm glad you agree with me that someone should have been tending those camels."

"Definitely."

"I'll tell you another thing," Dolly said, voice rising with spirit. "We're going to find out who is responsible for those horrid beasts and make them pay!"

"Agreed." Darby pointed up the canyon. "Isn't that a trail winding back up to the road?"

Dolly brushed strands of wet, plastered hair from her china-blue eyes. "Well, I suppose if you were a jackrabbit you might consider it a trail."

"I admit that it's not much, but I think it might be passable."

"I don't," Dolly argued. "We'd get halfway up and either the horse would balk and refuse to budge, or else the fool thing would panic again and send me to my death."

"You might be right," Darby sighed. "We'll keep moving until we find a better trail or reach the valley below."

To their surprise and relief, the canyon walls soon parted and grew gentle enough for them to climb up to the safety of their mountain road. Darby wiped perspiration from his brow and said, "My dear, we can either return to Carson City and report the loss of the horse and carriage to the liveryman, or we can continue on up to Lake Tahoe and send back word of our disaster later."

"Let's go on. It's hot down below and cool up at the lake.

Besides, we're already overdue and Bear and Zack might be getting worried."

"Not very likely," Darby said as he started up the road with the horse and Dolly in tow.

They had only traveled a mile before they were overtaken by a freight wagon driven by a little rooster named George. After Darby gave a quick explanation of their terrible ordeal, the driver offered them a ride on up to Lake Tahoe. George was very skinny with a tobacco-stained mustache and goatee. His Adam's apple bobbed as he talked, which was constantly. To Darby's mind, George was as chirpy as a bird but he and Dolly got along splendidly and chattered like long-lost friends.

"So," George said cheerfully when they saw the wagon wheel furrows that angled over the edge of the cliff, "this is where you met Mohammed, huh?"

"Is that the lead camel's name?"

"Sure! He's famous in western Nevada. And everyone in these parts knows that those camels travel this road every day like clockwork. Monday, Wednesday and Fridays they haul caskets of sweet Tahoe Lake water down to Virginia City and sell it damn near for the price of ale. Tuesdays, Thursdays, and Saturdays they bring coal and supplies up to the lake. Never fails. This is Wednesday, you see. That's why you ran into Mohammed. Huge, ugly critter. He spits green gunk at you and he's pretty damned accurate."

Darby looked down at his ruined black suit. His shirt, once white, had a big green stain that even the river had not been able to wash clean. "It was him all right. I'm surprised someone hasn't shot Mohammed long before now, he's so mean."

"I heard that *all* camels are mean," Dolly added.

"Oh, they are, miss! They're the most cantankerous, ill-mannered beasts you ever did see. They all kick and bite worse than mules or mustangs. And Mohammed, if he's really on the prod, will vomit at you."

George stuck a dirty forefinger down his throat and made a horrible face and disgusting sounds to emphasize his point.

"Ugggg," Dolly groaned. "How yucky!"

"Oh, he is that!" George agreed, looking pleased by the reaction he'd gained.

"Who controls him and the rest of the caravan of mangy camels?" Darby demanded. "I can't recall seeing anyone in the split second before we went flying over the side of this mountain."

"There's this little Arab fella named Emil. He loves those cussed camels. He totes around a big saber and an old Arabian blunderbuss. He'll fight to the death to save Mohammed or any of the other camels. About six months ago Emil up and chopped one miner's finger off for lighting a match to a sleeping camel's tail."

George belly-laughed, his shrill, womanish voice echoing across the lake. "Boy, it sure made that tall, ugly sucker get up and run!"

Despite their intense dislike for camels, neither Darby nor Dolly was one bit amused by such a cruel prank. Darby said, "He deserved to lose his finger for such a mean trick."

It wasn't the response that George had expected and his laughter suffered a lame death. He shifted uncomfortably on his seat and grumbled, "Yeah, well, a lot of folks in these parts feel different. I keep expecting to find that little Arab bugger strung up and every last one of his mangy camels shot."

"Does Emil own them?"

"Nope."

"Then who does?" Darby asked. "Because *that* is the person who will compensate us for our losses."

George frowned. "Mister, I'm afraid that'd be Big Bert Jasper. He's badger-mean. Bigger than a barn and uglier than the close end of these mules. He's scared more men to death with his face than Billy the Kid ever hoped to shoot."

George winked. "Mister, if you challenge Bert, you'd better kiss your lady goodbye."

Darby had heard this sort of talk before and scoffed. "If Bert refuses us fair compensation, I'm going to be his worst nightmare come true."

George was not impressed. No reason he should have been, because Darby looked to be just another eastern dandy making foolish talk. As for Darby himself, he knew that his pledge was not taken very seriously by the driver. Men always misjudged him for a big softie. How could they know that, underneath an inch of fat lay a mountain of hard muscle? Darby was only 5'10" but his weight, even when down to near skin and bone, was never under 225. Right now, it was a shade over 250 and he believed that very few men could have lifted a half-submerged carriage as he had done only a few hours earlier.

"Were I you," George advised, "I'd just write this wreck off as a bad experience. Tangling with Big Bert is just going to make things worse for you than they are already."

Darby looked to poor, battered Dolly. "Mister," he said, "you aren't me and I *live* for the moment when I come face to face with this Bert Jasper and his little Arab friend. And as for Mohammed, that two-humped monstrosity's days are numbered."

The freighter didn't say anything, but he still did not appear very impressed. When they finally crested the ring of mountains that cradled the jewel of Lake Tahoe, the freighter stopped and gave his mules a long blow.

"I always forget how beautiful this lake is," Darby said, studying the huge body of deep blue water ringed by emerald forest and towering peaks. "It's one of the most magnificent alpine lakes in the world."

Dolly linked her arm through Darby's. She inhaled deeply of the pines and snuggled up against him. "It's been a disastrous trip up from Carson City, but I think we should just put all that behind us now. There is too much beauty and peace here to be angry with anyone."

Darby's bushy eyebrows arched with surprise and his brow furrowed with displeasure. "What are you trying to say? That I should just forget about the wreck and those responsible for those stinking camels?"

She shrugged her shoulders and said, "Maybe. Why not?"

"Why not! Dolly, whoever owns those wretched camels is responsible for the loss of *The Glory Guns!* Furthermore, our carriage was destroyed, you almost drowned and a good horse was killed! We can't allow all that to pass."

"I know, it isn't right," Dolly said patiently. "But if this little Arab really is such a dangerous character and if Big Bert is even worse, I just don't think it's worth spilling blood over."

"It'll be *their* blood, not mine."

"Yes, dear," she said, patting his arm, "but why don't we just worry about finding Bear and Zack instead of seeking revenge at the first opportunity?"

Darby scowled. She was patronizing him and he didn't like that. On the other hand, Darby realized, there was nothing that could be done to replace his manuscript. And while it might feel good to drive his knuckles through Big Bert's and Emil's teeth, it really would not solve a thing.

"You're right," he conceded, "the first thing we have to do is find Zack and Bear. The sun will be going down in an hour or two."

"I know where them two old boar hogs are holed up," George offered.

"Where?"

"Right about the south end of the lake. Look for the most rickety old dock and the sorriest steamboat. They'll belong to Bear Timberly and Zack Woolsey. Either that, or close your eyes and follow your nose until your stomach flops."

Darby and Dolly exchanged meaningful glances. Darby said, "Pretty bad, George?"

"Bad?" The driver scoffed. "Let's just say that, among the misfits that work steamboats, Zack and Bear are in a class all by themselves."

This news did not really surprise Darby. He'd tangled with them years before when the two lovesick fools had abducted Dolly and taken her to Snakegrass Junction. Darby had had to rescue the poor woman. It had taken quite a while before

Darby had come to accept that the pair were full of mischief rather than meanness.

"If you are passing by their place," Darby said, "we would be extremely grateful for the ride."

"It's a little out of my way," the driver said, his voice taking on a crafty edge. "About five dollars' worth."

Darby reached into his pockets to discover that his wallet was missing, probably lost on his long tumble down into the river. All he had left was a few coins.

"Blast!"

"What's the matter?" Dolly asked. "No money?"

"I'm afraid not." Dolly had already informed him that her purse and all the money had been lost in the river.

"I'll take your pocket watch and that gold chain," George offered hopefully.

"Like hell you will. We'll walk first!"

"Then how about that bunged-up horse you tied to the back of my wagon?"

"Nope."

George lost his veneer of cheeriness and good will. His voice turned nasty when he said, "Mister, it'd be a long walk for a man your size and a woman."

"We're up to it," Dolly said, clearly outraged and disappointed by this sudden and disagreeable change of temperament. "Don't pay him, Darby! I don't mind riding the horse while you lead him to Zack and Bear's cabin."

Darby extracted the coins from his pockets. "This is all the money I have. Either take it or we walk."

George wasn't pleased but he could see that Darby wasn't bluffing. He snatched up the coins and jammed them into his coat pocket. They traveled the next few miles without further conversation.

THOUGH WARNED, neither Darby nor Dolly was quite prepared for the pathetic sight that greeted them at the waterfront. Bear and Zack's dock—if you could grace it by that description—was sagged badly on rotting pilings and most of the boards were either missing or busted. There was a windowless, ramshackle log cabin nearby guarded by two hounds with the size and dispositions of cornered cougars. Fortunately, they were chained to the front door.

"Zack and Bear must still be out on the lake," George remarked, unable to hide his relief. "Best I be getting along. What are you gonna do with that poor horse hitched on back?"

"Maybe feed him to those dogs," Darby said drily. "After all, he was one of the pair that sent us over the mountainside."

"Don't blame him," Dolly said as they climbed down from the wagon. "He'd probably never seen a camel before. Imagine how you'd feel if you didn't know such ugly things existed."

Darby tied the bay gelding to a ponderosa pine tree. He was furious about losing his wallet and all his money. Now, he'd have to telegraph his publisher for additional funds, and, given that his latest highly anticipated manuscript was irretrievably lost, they would not be pleased. At the very least, Mr. Warner would exact the promise of another manuscript in short order to satisfy the Derby Man's voracious readership.

Darby was not at all sure how he was going to explain to his friend and publisher that he might never be able to write again. He would have to explain that the loan would simply be an advance against future royalties on previously published books. Either that, or Darby could later withdraw money and repay the loan out of several very large deposits gaining interest in a couple of prominent New York banks. Either way, Darby was good for the money and the New York publishing house would simply have to understand that losing *The Glory Guns* manuscript had been like ripping out his heart.

The two fierce hounds continued to yap and growl, hackles up and teeth bared.

"Nice," Darby grumbled as he joined Dolly beside the decrepit dock.

She turned and called sweetly to the hounds, who ignored her and kept barking and snarling. "Oh," Dolly said, "don't mind them! They're just putting on an act!"

"An act?"

"Sure. They're trained to guard the cabin. Now, they can't very well do that if they wag their skinny tails at every stranger who comes by, now can they?"

"I suppose not," Darby said, knowing damn good and well the hounds weren't acting but were vicious as snakes.

He shaded his eyes and stared across Lake Tahoe, searching for the two mountain men. Unfortunately, the sun's glare off the water was blinding. The wind had picked up as it usually did in late afternoon and whitecaps danced and whirled across the lake. Over the sound of the barking hounds, seagulls screeched their displeasure at the fierce gusts of wind threatening to bat them into the pines.

Darby turned back toward the cabin. "Maybe Zack and Bear drowned on this rough water. Maybe they just went down like captains on a sinking ship."

Dolly frowned, making it plain that she didn't approve of Darby's gallows humor. "Just because this has been a completely rotten day doesn't mean you should talk like that. Besides, it could put a jinx on them."

"They're their own jinx," Darby said. He wished the hounds would stop their braying, which was beginning to grate on his already frayed nerves. "Dolly, we can't stay in that cabin. It's probably infested with lice, fleas and vermin. You know how slovenly Zack and Bear live."

"You're right," she said, "but we have no money. What choice do we have but to wait until Zack and Bear return, then move in with them until your publisher sends cash?"

"None."

Darby shrugged his massive shoulders. They were chafed and sore from lifting the half-submerged carriage. Tomorrow, he and Dolly would both ache from this day's punishing accident.

"I hope there's a telegraph office up here so J. Franklin can wire us plenty of money," Darby said.

"He'll do that without a manuscript?"

"Certainly. But until then, what a pathetic fix we're in! My cigars and French cognac were all lost in the river. I even had a bottle of champagne to celebrate our reunion with Bear and Zack."

"I know, I know," she said sympathetically. "But Zack and Bear would have guzzled it anyway. And darling, you know they'll have some good corn liquor in that cabin to cheer us up in a hurry."

"Either that or poison us."

"Look!" Dolly cried. "Isn't that them steaming toward us now?"

Darby helped Dolly make their way out to the end of the rotting dock. They stood balanced on the few solid boards and Darby squinted into the late afternoon sun. Sure enough, he could see a little steamboat busting through the waves. Moments later, he recognized the huge figure of Bear and, nearby, the thin but very tall form of Zack Woolsey. Their steam engine howled and black smoke was pouring from a rusty stack. The vessel was molten silver against the crimson canvass of a Sierra sunset.

"Crazy as ever," Dolly said as the boat grew larger and sounded as if it were ready to explode, "but they look like they are having fun."

It was true. As the boat closed on the dock, Darby could see that the pair were laughing and pulling on a jug. When they spotted Dolly and Darby waiting at their landing, they blasted a steam whistle in greeting. Despite himself, Darby had to ignore his own miserable circumstances and grin. Seeing the pair of old mountain men again and how much fun they were having brought back good memories. Zack and Bear were crazy as loons, but they had a rare zest for life and obviously still enjoyed good health though both men were probably on the sundown side of sixty.

"They ought to start slowing down their boat, shouldn't they?"

"I'd certainly think so."

But the pair did not. Instead, they kept their steamer at full throttle.

"Maybe they're just showing off," Dolly said, trying to hide her growing apprehension as she took a retreating step. "That's their style."

"I know," Darby said, as the steamer grew nearer and nearer. "And I think we'd better get off this dock right now!"

He spun around and started to run but crashed heavily through a rotting board. He dropped to his armpits in the freezing lake and badly barked both shins.

"Dolly" he bellowed, kicking and swearing as the steamboat bore down on them. "Help me out of here!"

Dolly bent over and tried to pull Darby up. She kept glancing up at the onrushing boat as Zack and Bear whooped and howled with devilish delight.

"Come on!" she grunted. She pulled with all her might as Darby ripped away boards in a desperate effort to extricate himself.

Somehow, he'd lost one of his shoes. He was soaked to the crotch and his pants were ripped halfway off. "Dammit, you old idiots!" he shouted, waving his fist in fury.

At the very last instant, Bear steered hard to the starboard and the vessel just missed the dock. Zack cut the throttle. The steam whistled and screamed and the boiler banged in violent protest as the vessel circled back out to the lake, gradually losing momentum. The pair of mountain men, laughing so hard they could barely stand upright, made a complete loop, then plowed the hull of their steamboat into the sandy beach and jumped out.

"Miss Dolly!" Bear shouted, coming on the run with Zack right behind.

Darby watched with ill-concealed fury as the three embraced and did a little dance on the shore. Nearby, the steam engine belched black smoke and soot, gave a tubercular cough and died.

"Well, well!" Zack said, his lean horse face covered with gray whiskers stained brown with tobacco juice. "If it isn't the Derby Man come to help his old friends!"

Darby managed a thin smile as he carefully made his way back to shore. "Stand back while I get off this sorry excuse for a dock!"

Zack's welcoming smile slipped. "Say there, what you got stuck in your craw this time? You look a little hard-used, friend!"

Darby shook hands with Zack, who was even leaner and taller than he'd remembered, then had to endure a hug from Bear Timberly, one of the few men who equaled Darby's girth and physical strength. Bear was grinning like a kid at his own birthday party and his eyes were shining with genuine happiness, causing Darby to momentarily forget his ruined clothes and lost manuscript. And even the hated camels and how he'd almost lost Dolly in the canyon river only a few hours earlier.

"It's good to see you both," he admitted. "It really is."

Zack and Bear beamed. "We got bunks for you in the cabin."

"I think we'll sleep outdoors."

"Naw! *We're* going to do that! You take our beds! Me and Bear are used to sleeping on the cold, hard ground. Besides, big fella, we got a bet going."

"On what?"

"On how many lice it'll take to lift you off either one of our tick mattresses!"

Zack jabbed his friend in the ribs and they both bent over laughing. Darby's expression was extremely pained. When the laughter finally subsided, he said in a hard, uncompromising voice, "I *insist* that we sleep outdoors. Is that understood?"

Zack and Bear stopped grinning. They knew when the Derby Man meant business and so they just nodded. Then

Bear clapped Darby on the shoulders hard enough to drop most men.

"We got a payin' job ferrying logs across this lake tomorrow and we could use some help. You and Miss Dolly want to come?"

"Sure," Dolly said brightly. "We'd love to help."

"What about you?" Zack asked, turning to Darby.

Darby wouldn't have dreamed of letting Dolly go out on Lake Tahoe alone with this pair of old crazies. "I wouldn't miss it."

"Good!" Bear shouted. "This calls for a real celebration!"

"Yes sir!" Zack proclaimed. "We'll do it up tall. Nice to have friends with money I always say."

"We haven't got any money," Darby informed the pair.

"What?" Their yellow smiles melted like rancid tallow in a cooking pot.

"You heard me. Dolly and I had a little accident on the way up here. We lost all our money and almost lost our lives."

"Oh," Bear said, recovering quickly. "Well, no matter. I guess we can celebrate after we get paid tomorrow."

"Yeah," Zack said without enthusiasm. "There ought to be enough money to buy a jug and some vittles."

He looked closely at Darby and Dolly. "You two gonna get some money pretty soon?"

Eager to get back at the pair, Darby shook his head. "I don't expect so. Do you, Dolly?"

"Probably not," she said, playing along with Darby's game.

Zack and Bear exchanged solemn glances. Finally, Zack cleared his throat. "No matter. We won't starve and that's for certain. Darby, you've always paid more than your share of the freight. It's time we did a little repaying."

Darby was impressed by their generosity but not really surprised. Despite their many shortcomings, Zack and Bear had always been willing to share whatever little they owned.

"We'll all do fine," Darby promised. He glanced down at his ruined suit. "But I need a bath, a shave, a new suit of clothing and a new pair of shoes."

"Might be a little hard," Zack offered. "There's only a couple of general stores close by and they don't carry suits. Prices are mighty high up in these mountains, and if you ain't got any money . . ."

Darby scowled. "Then take us to the nearest telegraph office and I shall set about rectifying our sad circumstances."

"I hope you mean to send for lots of money," Zack said.

"Enough," Darby replied, choosing his words carefully, "to take care of Miss Beavers' needs as well as my own."

"And not your old friends!" Bear sounded crushed.

"Maybe some," Darby hedged. "And while we are on our way, I want you to tell me where I can find a man by the name of Bert Jasper."

Bear scowled. "He's a bad one, Darby. What do you want to see a rattler like him for?"

"It's a long and very unfortunate story," Darby said, feeling very uncomfortable in his wet, torn pants. "And if you don't mind, I'd rather tell it to you on the way to town."

Zack and Bear nodded. They each took one of Dolly's arms and left the Derby Man to limp and squish along behind.

Three

WHEN DARBY AWOKE the following morning under a pine tree, he was stiff and cold. But the sun was floating over the rim of the ancient volcano that cupped Lake Tahoe like a goblet of sparkling champagne and the air was warming. Darby rolled over to stare at Dolly Beavers. Her lovely face still registered telltale hints of yesterday's near catastrophe. Her hair was tangled and there were dark circles under her eyes. Darby's hand reached out involuntarily to touch her cheek but he pulled it back, wanting her to sleep as long as possible.

When he sat up, the Derby Man felt an arrow pierce his brain and he stifled a groan. The rotgut whiskey that he and the mountain men had consumed last night had left its calling card. Darby cradled his head in his hands. He supposed, given the lateness of the hour, that Zack and Bear had long since steamed across the lake in order to fulfill that promised logging job.

Darby was wrong. When he shoved the tangle of his blankets aside and wobbled erect, he saw that the little steamer was still resting on the beach. There was no sign of life in the cabin and even the two vicious hounds guarding the door slumbered.

Darby stretched and knuckled the sleep from his eyes. His mouth tasted awful and his stomach fomented a revolt. If only he had one of his good Cuban cigars! It would do his constitution wonders. Lacking that, he stumbled down the beach to inspect Zack and Bear's steamboat.

It was a side-paddler about thirty feet long with a huge rusty boiler taking up most of the deck space. The deck was tangled with ropes and chains amid broken whiskey jugs. Darby noted a small bin of coal and some logs piled up near the firebox. The vessel's stern rested in the lake and it was flooded with several inches of water. Darby frowned to see that wads of moss had been wedged into a split seam. It did not take a veteran sailor to know that the entire vessel was in desperate need of caulking. The boat's deplorable condition was about what Darby had sadly expected.

Darby hopped out of the boat and turned his attention to the magnificent panorama of Lake Tahoe. The lake was more beautiful by far than any painting. The eastern shore was steeped in the shadow of the same mountains that he and Dolly had crossed the previous day. But the other edges were brilliantly colored by the stunning reflections of other mountaintops which bristled with rugged pines.

The water itself was so remarkably clear that Darby could easily distinguish rocks forty or fifty feet below the surface magnified as if under a powerful microscope. Overhead, huge cumulus clouds sailed like puffs of wind-blown cotton, their immense shadows darkening vast sections of sparkling water.

Darby knew that in the morning Lake Tahoe was like a sleeping infant—smooth-skinned and deceptively placid. But in the afternoon the infant usually awakened to a howling tantrum. When that happened, Lake Tahoe's surface would boil and froth. Bolts of lightning would spark wildly off the surrounding mountain peaks and the wind would screech like a banshee.

Darby's gaze was pulled back to the rickety side-wheeler.

"Mornin'!" a voice called in greeting.

Darby turned to see a man in his early seventies ambling in his direction. He bore a pleasant expression. His tanned face was weathered and he wore a baggy gray sweatshirt and a sailor's cap with shocks of white hair poking out underneath. Clenched between his teeth was a pipe belching smoke and sparks.

"Morning," Darby said, uncomfortable in the stiff new clothes he had managed to buy only after being forced to relinquish his gold pocket watch and chain as collateral.

"Fine morning to be out fishing," the cheerful gentleman said, coming up to stand before Darby then introducing himself as Boots even though he was wearing shoes. "You new in these parts?"

"I am."

"Yep. Saw you and that yellow-haired gal asleep when I first passed by at sunrise." Boots wagged his forefinger at Darby with disapproval. "Ain't right for such a pretty gal as that to have to sleep on the ground, you know. Makes even the best of 'em as stiff and cranky as old women."

"We're looking for a cabin to rent," Darby explained. "Until then, we are staying with Mr. Timberly and Mr. Woolsey."

At the mention of those names, Boots' lip curled with contempt. "Ha! Them lobo wolves ought to've been shot years ago. Now they're trying to take over the log-towin' business. But they don't know spit about this lake or steam engines. One day, they'll either get drunk and fall overboard and do the rest of us a favor, or they'll just get caught in a storm and sink."

Darby had to admit that his own assessment was pretty similar to that of this outspoken old man. However, Zack and Bear were his friends and he felt compelled to defend their character.

"They are really mountain men," Darby argued lamely. "Once they tamed the wilderness and trapped beaver. They can tell you stories of Kit Carson and Jim Bridger and the famous Rendezvous of the Rocky Mountain trappers."

"They're both stuffed to their ears with cow plop," Boots scoffed. "Too pickled in the brains to know fact from fiction."

Darby was beginning to get irritated. "Well," he said, "I never meant to imply that every word they spoke was the gospel."

"The truth is they've outlived their time—but then, so have I. Difference between us is that I know it and they don't.

When I first arrived at Lake Bigler—that's what they called it back then—there wasn't more than a handful of people around. We lived in peace with the Indians and worked the Truckee River and supplied the folks rushin' over these mountains to the big gold strike of '48. We sold 'em grass hay fresh cut in these mountain meadows. Kept their livestock alive."

"I'm sure you did, but . . ."

"And we sold 'em dried fish and pemmican we cured over our fires. And oxen yokes and handles for their axes that we carved with our knives and hatchets."

Darby nodded. He could see that this old man was going back in time, remembering the Forty-Niner Gold Rush. "Do you recall the tragedy of the Donner Party?"

"Hell yes! I helped bring what was left of them out." Boots' expression grew distant and wintery. "Them that didn't get stewed and eaten we hauled over to Sutter's Fort. Back then, old Captain Sutter had the world by the tail. He was richer than an Eee-gip-shun faro. Yes sir! Then he lost it all to drink and dissipation, like that pair of timber wolves you call your friends."

"They're just trying to make a living," Darby argued. "The beaver are all trapped out and they have to do something to feed themselves."

"Well, they won't do it here! They'll drown or get themselves murdered. Why, they're taking potshots at their competitor's boilers with those buffalo rifles!"

"Is that right?"

"Sure is!" Boots turned and stabbed a finger at the pitiful steamer. "That thing is an insult to a sailor. Look at the way those two treat her! Disgraceful even to a flatlander. I spent the last twenty years of my life rafting logs across these waters from sawmill to freight landings. I'm a *real* salt! That's why I get pukey just walking past this damned leaking boat."

"They're always a little short of money," Darby said.

"They're always a little short of brains!"

Darby had heard enough. "Excuse me," he snapped, turning and starting back toward Dolly.

"You take my advice," Boots yelled, "and you'll light out of here fast before you get yourselves in a bad fix with that pair of crazies! You take my advice . . ."

Boots didn't have a chance to shout more advice because Zack stepped into the doorway and cursed, then untied the two vicious hounds and yelled, "Sic 'em!"

The two hounds, which had been sleeping only an instant before, suddenly turned into ferocious, snarling beasts. They bounded across the yard and the old salt let out a whoop and took off running.

"Hey!" Darby protested with shock. "You can't let them hurt that man!"

"Aw," Zack grinned wickedly, "it's good for that windy old bastard to stretch hisself with a run before he enjoys a nice cold morning swim."

Darby wheeled around just in time to see Boots take a running dive into the lake. The old man stayed under almost ten seconds and when he surfaced, his arms were flailing like a windmill, propelling him out of reach of the hounds, who showed no interest in the frigid water.

Bear had appeared behind Zack and they both guffawed at the sight of Boots swimming for his life. Darby, however, was anything but amused. Furthermore, he was concerned that the hounds, once they realized they hadn't a chance of catching Boots, who was proving to be a remarkably good swimmer, would turn and attack him or Dolly.

Darby spotted a limb close by. He broke it over his knee and hefted it as the hounds bayed at the swimmer.

"What's the stick for?" Zack yelled.

"Those hounds!"

"Aw, they're used to you by now. You're their friends."

"Well, they haven't proven that to me," Darby said, "and until they do, I'll keep this stick handy."

The hounds soon gave up on Boots. The old man, after swimming about fifty feet out into the lake, turned and paralleled it until he finally came to another dock far up the shore-line. When he climbed out, he shook his fist and yelled things that Darby was glad Dolly could not hear.

That only made Zack and Bear laugh harder. They called their hounds and the beasts raised their hackles but did not test the Derby Man as they returned to the cabin.

"We'll fire up the pot and make us some coffee," Zack said.

"That would help," Darby replied. "Boots says that you and Bear are taking potshots at your competition. Is that true?"

"Aw, we're just havin' us a little target practice. Not tryin' to hit nothing much."

"Then it *is* true." Darby was appalled. "You can't operate a business like that! You've either got to compete or find an-other line of work. You can't scare off your competition."

"Why not?" Bear asked. "I mean, we're not trying to kill 'em or nothing."

Darby groaned. He really wasn't in the mood to argue with this pair.

"Let's get some coffee," Darby said. "And what about that job we were supposed to do early this morning?"

"We'll get to it soon enough," Bear grumbled, his eyes bloodshot. "Ain't no sense in working on a bad hangover, now is there?"

Darby saw that it was useless to argue. But of one thing he was quite sure, Zack and Bear were not well suited to the steamboat business.

"Why don't you wake up Dolly," Bear suggested as they started back inside the cabin. "We probably ought to be get-tin' across this lake."

"It's a little late in the day for that now, isn't it?"

"Hell, we got a good eight to ten hours of daylight," Zack argued. "Besides, we promised the mill that we'd deliver their logs today, come rain or shine."

Darby scowled. "All right, let's forget about the coffee and get that boiler fired up. The sooner we leave, the sooner we return."

Zack didn't look pleased. "Hell of a thing for a man to start to work without coffee. Especially when he suffers a hangover."

"You're getting soft," Darby said. He was not inclined to be sympathetic since his own brain was bursting. "I'll wake up Dolly and you chain those dogs. I want to be steaming across that lake in less than a half hour."

"Damn if you ain't a slave driver," Bear muttered.

Darby woke Dolly and by pushing hard, he soon had them steaming across the lake. The air was still very calm and Darby could see only a couple other steamboats on the water, both several miles away.

It took them two hours to get across the lake and then another hour to tie into a logging boom. They were supposed to drag about twenty big logs across and Darby doubted they could do it. When their chains first tightened on the big raft of logs, the little steamboat squatted down and wheezed pathetically. Bear fed the firebox until it grew cherry red and the steam whistled like an overheated teapot inside the rusty old boiler.

"If it blows," Darby said anxiously, "we are fish bait."

"Aw," Zack hollered over the din, "she ain't going to blow. This here boiler is as sound as the dollar and tighter than . . ."

Darby's menacing look stopped Zack's mouth. He glanced at Dolly and then he smiled. "Tighter than a tick feedin' on a fat dog, Miss Dolly!"

"Best get that wreckage moving in a hurry," a lumberjack shouted from the lagoon where the logs had been waiting. "Could be rough out there this afternoon."

"Only thing that's really rough is the men on this boat!" Bear shouted, raising a clenched fist.

The lumberjack snorted with derision and went back to his work. Darby and Dolly kept their silence as wood and coal both were thrown into the firebox and the steam pressure climbed to a dangerous level. Finally, they began to make headway.

So far, so good, Darby thought. With any luck, they would be across the lake within three hours, deliver the logs and be back in time for supper.

But that was not to be. Just over two hours later, the wind suddenly picked up, as always from the west. Darby and Dolly both looked anxiously at a line of ominous thunderclouds rushing toward them. Five minutes later, the wind was whipping the lake into a frothing frenzy. Their smooth progress ended as the steamer began to buck the waves. It was as if they were suddenly dragging a great sea anchor.

"We're barely making any progress!" Darby shouted over the screaming protest of both machine and nature. "We've got to unchain that log boom and get out of here!"

"Are you crazy!" Zack yelled. "That boom is worth more than this boat! We lose it out here and we'll never work for that lumber mill again!"

"Forget about money before we swamp and drown!"

"He's right!" Dolly cried. "Zack, you've got to release those logs! We can find them tomorrow morning after this storm has blown itself out!"

Zack exchanged glances with Bear. Bear nodded his head in agreement. He was hanging on the wheel and the stalled vessel was being pushed sideways by the wind and waves. If their little sidewheel paddle got fouled in a chain, they would be in an awful fix.

"All right!" Zack shouted, throwing a lever that stopped the paddle so that the chains could be freed. "Darby, you take the wheel. Once we get the chains off, give her power!"

Darby understood the importance of what Zack was saying. If they could make forward progress they had a chance, but if they were bogged down the waves would swamp them.

Dolly threw herself forward to reach the Derby Man's side. She looked badly frightened. Waves were crashing over the starboard side and drenching them with freezing water. The storm clouds were almost overhead now and they could hear the rumble of thunder and then the sharp crack of lightning. A moment later, they were being pelted with hail.

Darby cursed. The very last thing Dolly deserved was to have to endure another ordeal in freezing water, but here it was again. He raged at himself for allowing this to happen. He should have insisted that they wait until tomorrow and leave early. Had they done that, they would have completed the job while the lake was still calm. They'd be warm and safe with money in their pockets.

"Give 'er full throttle!" Bear shouted into the wind.

Darby opened the steam valve and their vessel lurched forward, its rickety paddle churning madly into the waves. For the first time, Darby noticed that he was standing in about four inches of water.

Bear grabbed the wheel. "Start bailing!"

"With what!"

"Yer derby!" Bear yelled.

Darby tore off his already ruined and shapeless derby. He fell to his knees and began to scoop like mad. The moss he had earlier seen wedged into the open seams of the deck was now floating. Waves were crashing over the sides of the boat and when it took a hard list to starboard, Darby glanced up to see that water had poured into the open firebox where Zack had been pitching wood.

The effect was instant and disastrous. A loud hissing sound was emitted from the firebox and white smoke poured out to scald their legs.

Dolly screamed. Bear and Zack cursed. Darby bailed and the steam pressure necessary to turn the paddles died.

"Holy hogfat!" Bear raged. "We're going to swamp!"

It was true. The sidewheel paddles ground to a halt and without power, the vessel began to drift and yaw dangerously with the wind. Wave after wave poured water over the sides and Darby gave up his bailing.

He surged to his feet. "It's going down! Tear off anything that floats and prepare to go into the water!"

"No!" Zack shouted, dropping to his own bony knees and cupping his hands to scoop like a wild man.

Bear did the same and Darby, shamed a little, followed suit.

All four of them bailed water like crazy but each time a wave breasted the sides, the water level inside raised a little. Darby tried to stuff a silk handkerchief into the gap between the seams. It appeared to slow the leak a little and for the next quarter hour as the wind and waves battered and bullied them toward the south shore, they almost held their own.

At last, however, the water was so deep that the steamer began to wallow like a dying whale. Its rusty boiler popped and hissed as it cooled and when Darby looked up, he saw that they were less than a quarter mile from shore.

He gripped the large spoked wheel. It was bolted down solidly, but the Derby Man's neck slipped into his torso and his massive arms corded with a supreme effort. With his lips pulled back from his teeth, a tremendous groan was torn from his mouth an instant before he wrenched the wheel free.

"What the hell did you do that for?" Zack raged.

"It'll float and we can hang on to it until we are driven up on the shore."

"Maybe this boat'll reach the shore before we sink!"

Darby hoisted the wheel overhead. "Not a chance," he hollered even as the steamboat began to sink. Darby threw the wheel overboard, grabbed Dolly and, together, they jumped.

They grabbed the floating wheel and clung to it. "Come on!" Darby shouted. "There's room for all of us!"

Zack and Bear, up to their knees in water and with the steamer sinking beneath their feet, jumped for the wheel before the wind drove it out of their reach.

When the pair were clinging to the wheel, they twisted around and watched as their steamboat slowly disappeared. They all stuck their heads under the clear water and watched it drift out of sight. Darby had heard that the lake was extremely deep; now he was a believer. When they lifted their faces out of the water and rested their chins on the wheel, it was a sad moment, even though the vessel had long since outlived its usefulness.

Darby patted Zack on the shoulder. "You weren't meant to

be sailors, either of you. Maybe it's for the best. At least we're going to be safe."

Zack started to say something but then he cocked his head into the wind, listening hard. "Do you hear that?"

Darby listened intently and so did Bear and Dolly. The Derby Man could hear something. At first, he thought it was just the howl of wind across the water, then he wasn't sure. "Yes, I do hear something, but what is it?"

"Sounds . . . sounds like someone laughing," Dolly said.

"Yeah," Bear said. "But what . . ."

"Look!" Zack roared, swinging around and pointing toward the beach. "It's him! It's Boots and he's laughing!"

Darby unlocked one arm from the wheel and twisted around to see the old man jumping up and down on the beach, hollering, whooping, laughing and doing a little jig.

Zack's face paled and his voice shook with rage. "I'll feed that old geezer to the hounds tonight! I swear I will!"

It was crazy, even juvenile, but Darby felt an uncontrollable urge to share this last laugh with Boots. However, he decided that would be neither wise nor healthy.

Four

"JUST LOOK at those poor, sad dears," Dolly lamented, sweeping clouds of dust out the cabin door. "Since they lost that leaky old steamer Zack and Bear act as if their world has ended."

Darby, reclining in an axe-hewn chair beside the cabin, and the hounds, who had undergone some major attitude changes thanks to the toe of Zack's swinging boot, followed Dolly's eyes down to the shore. It had been two days since the side-wheeler had sunk in the lake and the mountain men were still moping.

"I suppose they owed money on that termite trap?"

"About five hundred dollars," Dolly said. "And they have other bills."

"That means that they'll soon skip out of this part of the country," Darby said, his own mood black because he still found it difficult to accept the loss of *The Glory Guns.* Furthermore, he was a man who did not wear the mantle of poverty with grace or good spirit.

"Hello the cabin!"

The dogs, whose names were Sid and Slick, came to their feet snarling and snapping at the ends of their chains. Darby went to see who had come to visit.

"You the Derby Man?"

"Yes."

The young, gangly man on the mule opened a leather pouch tied to his saddle. "This here telegram come all the way from New York City."

Darby's spirits soared. "It's from J. Franklin Warner," he said with great relief. "My publisher has sent help just in the nick of time."

Darby signed for the telegram and tore it open as its deliveryman, clearly disappointed in not receiving a substantial tip, rode away.

Dolly leaned forward expectantly. "What does it say?"

"How much did he send?" Bear asked, his small, deep-set eyes wide with excitement.

Darby ignored them and unfolded, then smoothed the telegram out and began to read aloud. "DEVASTATED YOU HAVE LOST THE GLORY GUNS. STOP. REWRITE AS SOON AS POSSIBLE. STOP. HAVE WIRED MONEY TO THE BANK OF NEVADA, VIRGINIA CITY. STOP. NEW BOOK CONTRACT FORTHCOMING. STOP. BUCK UP, BUCKINGHAM!"

Darby scowled. "Blast! Why didn't J. Franklin send the money to the bank up here!"

"Well," Dolly offered, "it really isn't much of a bank. Just a cabin with a vault no bigger than a trunk. Maybe it's too small to be known back in New York City."

"Maybe," Darby grumped. "At any rate, it's clear that we are going to have to visit the Comstock Lode to avoid starvation. I just wish J. Franklin had told me how much money he's sending."

"It'll be a lot," Dolly said confidently. "After all, you've often told me how you're their most successful writer. They'll have to take good care of you."

"Yes," Darby said, thinking that the New York publishing house would drop even him if they were convinced that the Derby Man would never write again. "It's just that it will be hard on everyone when they realize that I don't intend to ever write again."

"But why in tarnation can't you write anymore?" Zack asked.

"It's a long story." Darby managed a smile. "One I really don't think you'd fully understand."

Zack looked at the others. It was clear by his expression

that Darby's words did not sit well with him. He turned back to Darby. "Why don't you try me?"

"Yes," Dolly said, "I'd like to hear your reasons again too. Maybe I'll understand them better this time."

Darby knew he was trapped. To refuse any explanation would insult all three and Darby wanted to avoid that even though he was sure he could not possibly make his friends understand the illogic of a creative mind.

"I feel cheated and devastated by the loss of *The Glory Guns*. I can't possibly write another story as good. But even more important, creating a legend like Durango is like birthing a child. And then losing him . . . well, that's something only a mother who has lost a child might possibly understand."

"Who the hell is Durango?" Zack snapped. "Some kid or something?"

"No! Of course not," Darby snorted. He looked to Dolly for help.

"Durango," she explained, "is Darby's latest western hero. He's a fictional character. Brave. Handsome, savage and extremely violent."

"He's not *that* violent," Darby said.

"Well, from what you've told and read to me, he seems pretty violent to me. But he doesn't really like shooting men. Not very much, anyway."

Darby groaned. "Durango doesn't like killing at all!"

"That's what I said!" Dolly pursed her lips in concentration. "It's just that he is quicker on the hammer than anyone he faces."

"The trigger. Quicker on the trigger."

"That too," Dolly said agreeably. "I think he just likes to fondle his beautiful, pearl-handled revolvers."

"Pearl-handled revolvers!" Zack exclaimed. "What kind of a fella would strut around with a pair of fancy hawglegs like that! Any real self-respecting gunfighter would laugh hisself to death if he saw such a dandy!"

Bear began to chortle.

Darby flushed with anger and humiliation. "Never mind! I regret trying to explain any of this. I should have known better."

"Now, now," Dolly soothed, "I just think that you owe yourself, your publisher friend and all your fans an honest try at writing another dime novel."

Darby waved his hand in disagreement. "There is no point in arguing. What we need to do is go to the Comstock Lode and collect my money. Afterward, I'll pay Bert Jasper a visit. And we've still got that livery horse from Carson City to return as well as an explanation to make to the owner about the wreck of his carriage and the loss of his other horse."

"It sounds like a very unpleasant trip," Dolly said.

"Yes," Darby replied, "but there is no sense in putting the matter off any longer. We'll leave first thing tomorrow morning."

Bear said, "You'll need some backup when you face Big Bert."

"That's right," Zack said. "He's been known to have a few hangers-on who are also mighty quick with the gun."

Darby was afraid that his two old friends might cause more trouble than good in Virginia City. However, at the prospect of collecting New York money, their spirits were so much improved that Darby hadn't the heart to insist they remain at Lake Tahoe.

They left early the next morning on four scrawny saddle horses. Zack and Bear mumbled something about their being "borrowed." Having no one stupid or brave enough to feed Sid and Slick, the two hounds were allowed to tag along with the battered carriage horse.

Their journey down the mountainside was reasonably uneventful and when they arrived at the place where their carriage had crashed over the mountainside, they all dismounted to gawk at the wreckage far below.

"Hell of a fall," Zack observed. "You're both lucky to be alive."

"Darby saved me from drowning," Dolly said proudly.

"Anything left under that carriage that might be worth going down there after?" Bear asked.

"No," Darby said. "Except that my wallet and Dolly's purse are resting somewhere in that river."

"Might be worth hunting for," Zack said, reading his partner's thoughts. "We can do that on the way back."

"It's damn sure worth a look," Bear agreed. "But if we find it, half of the Derby Man's money is ours."

He turned to Dolly, looking a little embarrassed. "We wouldn't keep *your* money."

"How generous of you," she said pleasantly.

Darby ground his teeth in silence, then watched as Bear unearthed a sheet of manuscript paper that had been almost completely buried under dirt and manure.

"Well, look at this!" Bear exclaimed, turning to Darby. "Does it belong to you?"

"Yes," Darby said, taking the paper and shaking the dirt off. He stared at the page, a strong current of distaste in his mouth because of the green stain that violated his sacred prose. Even so, he could not help but read a few lines, enough to learn that this was from the action scene where Durango had been thrown into a snake pit. Darby studied his own neat handwriting until a rage boiled up inside him. But instead of balling the offending page up and hurling it off the mountainside, he jammed it into his pocket.

Dolly touched his arm. "It's a start," she whispered.

"Come along," Darby said, mounting his horse. "I'd like to get a hotel room in Virginia City tonight. But first, we have to get to the bank and get my money before it closes at five."

"And return this horse to the liveryman in Carson City," Dolly reminded him.

"Yes."

THEY REACHED CARSON CITY about noon and while Bear and Zack bought a couple of pounds of rotting mule meat for Sid and Slick, as well as some tins of sardines and a sack of soda crackers for themselves, Darby and Dolly sought out the livery owner.

"I'm afraid that I have some very bad news for you, Mr. Walter," Darby said, handing the man a lead rope attached to his scraped-up gelding.

Walter hardly recognized his poor horse. "What happened to him!"

Darby explained all about the camels and the accident and ended by saying, "It's a miracle that any of us are alive."

Walters, a barrel-chested young man in bib overalls, turned livid with anger. "Well, you're responsible, Mr. Buckingham! You rented the carriage and you agreed to bring it and the horses back in good shape!"

"Don't raise your voice at me," Darby warned. "I promise you will be fully reimbursed."

Walter deflated a little. "All right," he snapped, "let's see. The carriage was worth two hundred and the dead horse at least fifty dollars. The harness another fifty dollars. So that's three hundred even." Walter shoved out his hand. "The money, Buckingham."

Darby ignored the extended palm. "You'll get your money, but not from me."

"What the hell is that supposed to mean?"

"It means that Bert Jasper is the one who was responsible since it was his camels that caused the wreck."

"But *you* rented the carriage!"

Darby had to admit that he did bear at least a part of the responsibility for the loss. "All right, we're on our way to Virginia City right now and we ought to be back through tomorrow. I'll get the money from Jasper and pay you then."

"Uh-uh," Walter said, shaking his head vigorously. "I know Big Bert and the only thing you'll get from him is an ounce of lead through the gizzard. No sir! I want my money now!"

"Tough," Dolly said. "Between us we don't have a whole dollar. So you're just going to have to wait."

Walter's cheeks blew out and he balled his fists and started to curse. But Darby grabbed him by the shirtfront with his left hand and hoisted him aloft to the very tips of his toes.

"Don't say another word," the Derby Man warned as he cocked back his right fist. "Not if you value your front teeth."

Walter's eyes bugged and he had a dramatic change of heart. "Why, no sir!"

"Good," Darby said. He eased the man back down and smoothed out the wrinkles he'd made in Walter's shirt.

"Good luck, Mr. Buckingham," Walter said, swallowing noisily.

"Thank you."

Dolly linked her arm through Darby's and as they walked away, she gushed, "You were just wonderful, Darby! So convincing!"

Darby allowed himself a tight smile and said, "There are times when actions do speak much louder than words, my love. And this was one of those times."

THEY LEFT CARSON CITY following the Virginia & Truckee Railroad line east toward the barren hills and mountains where the biggest bonanza in the history of the West had been discovered in 1859, just when the California Gold Rush was going bust. The town had received its name when prospector "Old Virginny" James Finney had galloped through the sage and tumbled drunkenly from his horse. Shattering a full bottle of whiskey on the rocky ground, he'd crawled to his feet and shouted with great dignity, "I hereby christen thee Virginny City!"

The name had stuck and now Virginia City and its smaller neighbors, Gold Hill and Silver City, could boast of a population of over eleven thousand miners, prostitutes, gamblers, grocers, gunmen, merchants and thieves. The Comstock Lode was a magnet that attracted fortune hunters from around the world. It was wild, profane and great fun if a man didn't mind playing it fast and easy with cards, women and his life.

After leaving the heat of the high desert, Darby and his

companions rode up Gold Canyon, passing first through Silver City, then the little settlement at Devil's Gate, where they
were forced to pass between a narrow gateway of towering
rocks and pay a toll before entering Gold Hill.

Gold Hill was growing almost as fast as Virginia City. The
first time that Darby had visited the Comstock, Gold Hill had
consisted of nothing but canvas tents and other makeshift
dwellings constructed of blankets, potato sacks and even old
shirts sewn together, many stretched across brush or empty
whiskey barrels, rocks or broken wagon parts. Other early
miners had chosen to burrow dugouts in the hillsides and
competed for shelter with scorpions, rattlers and centipedes.
But now Gold Hill was a prominent Nevada city. It could
boast of its own newspaper, the *Gold Hill News*, which rivaled
Virginia City's colorful *Territorial Enterprise*, as well as a bank,
several hotels, barber shops, saloons, a public school, a Ma-
sonic lodge and three active fire companies.

As they passed through town, they saw a large banner
urging everyone to attend a picnic that would raise money for
street lamps and a publicly owned water company. No doubt
about it, Gold Hill was on the move.

After Gold Hill, the canyon became very steep. Their
horses really had to hump to climb the last mile and top the
Divide, a crest that separated Gold Hill from its larger and
more famous sister, Virginia City.

"Let's give these horses a breather," Darby said, moving
off the corkscrew road leading over the Divide. Even Sid and
Slick, their tongues lolling, showed no inclination to attack
the road.

Bear and Zack studied the bustling town and talked in low
tones, chuckling about some prositute or dance hall girl they
hoped to visit. But Dolly was much more serious because the
camels were on her mind.

"According to George, we should have met that camel caravan along the road between here and Lake Tahoe. Why do
you suppose we didn't?"

"I don't know," Darby said. "The same question crossed my mind."

Darby reached for his pocket watch, then remembered that he'd had to use it for collateral. Disgusted, he glanced up at the afternoon sun and judged it to be near four o'clock. "Let's find the bank and get my money before it closes. I can take care of Bert Jasper afterward."

Dolly nodded, trying to hide her worry. Everyone that she'd talked to said that Big Bert was an extremely dangerous fellow. Dolly was not afraid of him beating Darby Buckingham, but she was concerned that he or his friends might gun poor Darby down if things got out of hand. Dolly resolved that, while Darby was in the bank getting his money, she would have a little talk with Bear and Zack to ensure that the pair of old boars did not immediately get drunk in one of Virginia City's dozens of saloons or go off visiting the back street ladies. A few minutes later, they found the bank without difficulty, as almost all of them were located on C Street.

"This shouldn't take but a few minutes," Darby said, a trifle self-conscious that he had to conduct business in the only rough, ill-fitting clothes he could find at Tahoe's general store. Darby consoled himself with the thought that, with the money he was about to collect, he could purchase a new suit, clean himself up and become presentable again. Upon his return to Lake Tahoe, he would immediately reclaim his gold watch and chain.

Inside the bank, Darby asked to see the president and was told the man was out sick. "Then introduce me to your vice president."

"His name is Mr. Gerald Gloster. And your name?" the ascetic-looking clerk with the green eyeshade asked.

"Buckingham. Darby Buckingham."

"Yes sir."

A moment later, the vice president appeared. "Mr. Buckingham?" he asked skeptically.

"That's right." Darby shifted uncomfortably in his poor working man's clothes and the worn-out Indian moccasins that Bear had loaned him. "Mr. Gloster, I believe that you have some money that was wired to me by my New York City publisher."

"Of course," the vice president said. "We were expecting you but . . ." His voice trailed off as his eyes surveyed Darby's moccasins with obvious distaste. "We were expecting someone quite different."

Darby forced himself not to lose his temper. "Sometimes we all become victims of circumstances beyond our control, Mr. Gloster. But that is not the issue here. I want my money —now."

Gloster blinked. "Of course. I'll get the check."

Darby fidgeted under the scrutiny of the bank employees and customers, who must have thought he looked like an odd duck indeed with his rough shirt, worn moccasins and shapeless derby.

Darby's hand automatically wandered to where his vest pocket should have been for a cigar he couldn't yet afford to buy. With irritation, he dropped both hands into his lap and laced his pudgy fingers, tips resting on the wedge of knuckles long since flattened during his years of bare-knuckled brawling.

It took Gloster an inordinately long time to return with the check, and when he handed it to Darby he said rather stiffly, "You understand, of course, that we will need some identification before we cash this check."

But Darby didn't hear a word Gloster said. He had torn the envelope open and was staring at the check. "Three hundred dollars? Three hundred measly dollars!"

"Mr. Buckingham," Gloster pleaded. "Control yourself!"

Darby ground his teeth together and forced himself to read the short telegram that had accompanied the check. DEAR DARBY. STOP. HOPE THIS SUFFICES. STOP. WILLING TO ADVANCE FIVE THOUSAND ON SIGNING OF NEXT BOOK CONTRACT. STOP. PLEASE SEND TITLE, OUTLINE AND FORWARDING ADDRESS. STOP. NEED MANUSCRIPT WITHIN THREE MONTHS. STOP. GOOD LUCK! STOP.

Darby balled up the message and hurled it across the bank lobby. "Mr. Gloster, I want cash and I want it right now!"

Gloster took a mincing backstep. "But we will need some identification, Mr. Buckingham. It's for your protection, really. And . . . well," he stuttered, his nerve snapping like twine, "perhaps that won't really be necessary after all. I mean . . . it's obvious that you've had a few setbacks and . . ."

Vice President Gloster turned and fled to his office, yelling over his shoulder, "Endorse the check and give it to my cashier, sir!"

Darby scratched his name on the back of it, still outraged that his dear, trusted friend and publisher, Mr. J. Franklin Warner, would send such a piddling amount of money to his most famous dime novelist. Under any other circumstances, Darby would have shredded the check and sent it back with a stinging rebuke. But because his present circumstances were indeed bleak, he had no choice but to swallow his pride and cash the insulting check.

Moments later, Darby stormed out of the bank. He would find Bert Jasper and not only get reimbursement for the carriage and dead horse, but also for his lost manuscript. Either that, or he would extract payment out of the camel owner by brute force.

Five

"DID YOU get the money?" Bear asked.

"How much?" Zack wanted to know.

Dolly, however, read Darby's grim expression and said, "Not as much as you'd expected, right?"

Darby's voice shook with anger. "J. Franklin sent me just three hundred lousy dollars!"

The expectant grins worn by the mountain men slipped badly. "Well," Zack said after a moment, "that's still a whole lot better than a poke in the eye."

"Sure is," Bear said, trying to hide his disappointment. "We can get ourselves rooms, whiskey and have a high old time in Virginia City for a couple of days up here on three hundred."

"Not very likely," Darby said, untying his horse. He did not care much for horses, and this animal was no exception. It laid its ears back when Darby mounted and would have bitten him except that Darby had learned to keep his rein on the off side pulled up short.

"Let's find Bert Jasper," he said.

"That's easy," Zack replied, sniffing the air like a big grizzly. "We just follow the smell of camel."

Big Bert Jasper's camel yard was located out on D Street past the red light district and the V & T Railroad depot. From a distance, it could best be described as a stockade with high rock walls and a big double-gated entrance.

"Sid and Slick smell 'em already," Bear said. "That's why they're getting all worked up."

"Just keep those dogs leashed and under control," Darby ordered. "I'd like to keep this meeting peaceful."

"Ha!" Zack barked. "When you tell Big Bert Jasper that you want money, all hell's gonna break loose."

Now Darby could smell the camels. "Exactly where are the beasts?"

"Jasper keeps 'em penned up behind them big old high fences," Zack explained. "He's not afraid of any one man but he worries that the city council will outlaw camels within the city limits because they raise such a ruckus with other livestock."

"If he doesn't pay me fair compensation," Darby warned, "he'll have himself a *real* ruckus."

Sid and Slick were going crazy on the ends of their chains. "They hate those camels," Bear said. "I can't change that. You see, they had a little run-in with Mohammed and his friends about six months ago."

"What happened?"

"Mohammed won the first round. Got 'em both in the eyes with his green spit and then kicked 'em damn near across the lake. Poor Sid and Slick howled and howled. Musta hurt like crazy. Them are the fightingest dogs I ever did see. They mean to get even, even if it kills 'em."

Darby had more important matters of concern than two stupid hound dogs looking to get even. As they approached the yard gate, he could see four or five rough-looking men sharing a jug.

Zack scowled. "Darby?"

"What?"

"Why don't you let me and Bear handle this? We know Big Bert and can probably work things out peaceably."

"Not a chance. Is that him?"

"Yeah," Zack said. "Huge, ain't he."

Big Bert ought to have been named Big Tree, or Big Man Mountain because he stood at least six and a half feet tall and easily weighed three hundred pounds. His face commanded even more fear than his size because it was badly scarred by fire. It was blotchy, bright red in some places, bone white in others. His lips were fused at one end with scar tissue. Tufts of beard erupted from his jowls. He was speaking to his companions from the open side of his mouth.

Darby gulped. He had never seen such a frightening-looking human being. Bert Jasper looked like some creature who had been roasted then released from hell. He wore a pair of filthy buckskins that made Bear's and Zack's greasy leathers look clean by comparison. Instead of moccasins, Bert wore high-heeled boots and a sixgun with notches carved conspicuously on the walnut handle.

Darby heard Dolly's sharp intake of breath, then her plea, "Let's get out of here!"

The Derby Man forced himself to ignore the woman, while at the same time realizing that he might have finally bitten off more than he could chew. Darby kicked his horse a little out in front of his companions.

Sid and Slick were rumbling in their throats and, seeing them, Jasper shouted, "If them dogs go after my camels, I'll shoot 'em before they can reach the corral!"

"Control them!" Darby ordered.

"That's far enough," Jasper ordered as he and his men came to their feet. "What the hell is this, the Chamber of Commerce welcomin' committee?"

"Darby," Dolly pleaded, "let's forget about what we are owed and get out of here!"

"Not a chance." Darby reined his horse up and dismounted. Zack and Bear did the same. Sid and Slick fought their lead ropes, frantic to streak across the yard and attack the camels, which, led by Mohammed, were issuing their own squawking challenge.

"I understand you own those camels, Mr. Jasper," Darby said.

"That's right. You want to hire 'em?"

"No. They caused a wreck on the way up to Lake Tahoe. My fiancée, Miss Dolly Beavers, was almost killed. A good horse *was* killed. Our carriage was ruined and we barely escaped with our lives."

"That's a real shame, fella. Would have been a pity to lose such a handsome woman." Bert winked lasciviously. "Hey, pretty woman, you want to drink a little whiskey with us? Have a little fun? Huh?"

Darby's cheeks flamed. Dolly grabbed his arm. "Please!"

But Darby shrugged her aside. "You owe Mr. Walter, proprietor of the Carson Livery, three hundred dollars for a horse, harness and carriage. You owe *me* the loss of *The Glory Guns* and you owe Miss Beavers a sincere apology."

Jasper snarled, "I don't owe any of you doodly jack!"

"In that case," Darby said, dismounting and rolling up his sleeves, "I think you had better prepare to defend yourself."

"What!"

Darby kept rolling up his sleeves. "You heard me. I'm going to beat you to your knees and *then* you're going to pay me what is owed."

One of Jasper's friends reached for a gun but when the big bore of Zack's Hawken rifle came on line with his chest, he froze. Bear's rifle settled on the giant. "If any of your boys touch their guns, Jasper, I'll blow a hole in you big enough for Mohammed to shuffle through."

The giant's scarred cheeks turned beet red. "You sonofabitch, you'll pay for this!"

"Not likely," Bear said, the buffalo rifle rock steady in his big fists.

One of the men standing beside Jasper hissed, "What do you want us to do, boss?"

"Nothin'," Jasper whistled out the side of his mouth.

He turned his attention to Darby, who was just finishing with his sleeves and had raised his thick fists in a fighting stance. The Derby Man crouched and his shoulders humped.

"You are a joke, fat man. Do you think I am going to toe the mark and fight according to the Marquis of Queensberry rules?"

Darby's black mustache bristled. "No holds barred, sir. Just remove your weapons and let's see how tough you really are."

The giant yanked his pistol and then his knife free and set them on the porch. He balled his fists. They were the size of parlor pillows but as hard as anvils.

Darby stood his ground. In all his years of bare knuckle fighting, he'd never relied on guile or trickery to win a fight, and even though he was slightly past his best years, Darby knew he still packed a tremendous wallop with either hand. He was gifted with a knockout punch that no man could stand up against—not even a giant.

Jasper's expression was contemptuous as he rolled his sleeves up to reveal a pair of massive forearms. Very few sober men had ever had the nerve to face a giant. It was for that very reason that the Derby Man hoped that Jasper hadn't needed to refine his fighting skills. He was betting that Jasper had always either scared his opponent witless, or clubbed them to the floor with one or at most two blows.

With mocking laughter, Jasper lumbered forward and aimed at Darby's face. The eastern dime novelist ducked and his own muscular arm drove upward, catching Jasper just below the ribs. It was a thundering punch and the giant was lifted two inches off the ground.

Jasper staggered, then he reached down and scooped up a handful of dirt and hurled it into Darby's eyes before he could shield them. Darby felt a tremendous blow knock him flying. He crashed over a hitch rail and slammed into the freight office. For a moment, he was too dazed to get to his feet, but Jasper did it for him. The giant grabbed Darby by the shirtfront, measured his blow and drove his fist toward Darby's nose.

The Derby Man threw his head to one side and felt the giant's knuckles graze his cheek. He could heard his friends shouting for him to break loose before the giant took his head off with another punch. Darby struggled. His own massive arms came up and he grabbed Jasper by the ears and almost tore them from the giant's skull.

"Owww!" Jasper yelled.

Darby stomped the giant's foot and only after Jasper showed no reaction did Darby remember he was wearing a pair of damned moccasins. By then, Jasper had punched him so hard that his head was spinning.

Jasper roared and threw the Derby Man back against his office. He measured his blow and unleashed a thundering right cross. Darby slipped the punch and the giant's hand crashed through the wood siding. Before Jasper could tear it free, Darby stepped around behind the man and punished the giant's kidneys, each blow causing Jasper to grunt with pain.

The Derby Man stepped back and drove a murderous left hook to the point of the big man's jaw. Jasper struck the office so hard it shook to its foundations. His eyes glazed and he tried to shake off the effects of the stunning blow but Darby threw an overhead right to his cheek that split it to the bone. Jasper bounced back against the wall, batting at his face. When he saw his palm covered with his own blood, his eyes betrayed the first rat nibbles of fear.

"The money," Darby demanded, backing away and giving the giant a chance to save himself further punishment. "I want fair compensation."

Jasper lowered his head like a billy goat and charged. Darby dropped to the ground and swung his right leg at the giant's exposed left knee. Jasper howled and lurched badly. He attempted to regain his balance but he couldn't maneuver because his knee refused to bend.

Darby came up swarming. He had always been blessed with power and speed and now his fists rained on the giant from all angles.

Jasper grunted and rocked backward with every blow as he retreated. He tried to mount his own attack but as a former bare knuckles champion, the Derby Man had learned that, to finish a fight, you had to press your advantage. Darby now fought as if he were losing instead of winning. He didn't give Jasper a chance.

"Hit him!" Zack screamed.

"Whip him!" Bear shouted.

Darby took no pleasure in destroying another human being, even one as cruel and vicious as Bert Jasper. His heavily scarred knuckles blurred like the driving pistons of a locomotive. He fought like a professional, his punches short and brutal. Methodically, like a lumberjack felling a giant pine, he worked the body until Jasper crumpled and lowered his guard, then he drove bone-crunching blows to the giant's face.

Jasper tried to cover himself top and bottom but Darby's fists broke through his clumsy guard until the giant collapsed, pleading for mercy.

Darby stepped back, chest heaving, knuckles bloody and barked.

"I want repayment and I want an apology for Miss Beavers," he gasped. "Nothing more, nothing less."

"I don't *have* any money!" the giant sobbed. "Not more than a few dollars!"

Darby grabbed the man by the collar and shook him. "You're lying!"

"No! I swear it!"

Darby balled his fist and struck Jasper in the side of the face so hard the man flopped over backward and tried to crawl away.

Darby grabbed his boots and held him. "The money!"

"I don't have any!"

"He . . . he's telling you the truth!" one of the hardcases under guard shouted. "We're almost broke."

Darby released the man's boot and Jasper scuttled away on hands and knees.

"Mister," the man explained, "all Big Jasper owns is in those goddamn camels and their saddles. I swear it!"

"You're lying to me."

"No! Jasper got himself a contract with the Consolidated Mining Company. He was going to make a fortune off them camels starting next week! That's why Jasper fired Emil and quit the Lake Tahoe run."

Darby marched over to Jasper, who had crawled to a water trough and was dunking his head in the water. When he raised it, Darby saw that the giant's eyes were fast swelling shut.

"You owe Mr. Walters three hundred dollars and you owe me for my lost manuscript. And most important of all, you owe Miss Beavers an apology."

"I apologize, goddammit!" Jasper screeched. "I apologize!"

Dolly jumped from her horse and tried to pull the Derby Man back to his own mount. "Let's get out of here!"

But Darby shook his head. "No! That manuscript was worth tens of thousands of dollars! I refuse to let this man off after his causing us so much grief and expense."

"But he's broke!"

"How can that be!" Darby shouted with exasperation. "He owns this freight yard, that wagon, those camels and . . ."

"No I don't!" Jasper cried. "All I own are the camels. Take 'em!"

"What?" Darby did not want to believe that he had heard the giant correctly.

"Take 'em!" Jasper looked up, his ruined face suddenly transformed by some inner joy. "You heard me, they've been a curse! They're all I own and now they're yours, damn your eyes!"

"I won't have them!"

The giant cackled. He sounded demented. "Then let them all starve!"

And with that, Jasper climbed unsteadily to his feet and stumbled across the yard and through his gate. Darby was helpless as the giant brokenly weaved his way on up the road toward the saloons on C Street.

Darby stared, then yelled, "Hey, you can't just leave like this!"

In reply, Big Bert Jasper cackled hysterically and kept moving.

Darby whirled around to face the giant's drinking companions. "This yard, this shack . . ."

"Rent's overdue on all of it," one of the men said with a mocking sneer. "Good luck with those accursed camels. I wish I could be here when Mohammed realizes the hay is gone and he's got you to thank for it."

The rough-looking men all started for the gate wearing smug, goading expressions.

"Hold it!" Zack warned. "Stop or . . ."

"Let them go," Darby said. "We can't just shoot them all in the back."

"But . . . but what the hell!" Bear shouted in anger and helpless frustration. "Jasper *owes* you!"

Darby shook his head in bewilderment as Mohammed squawked and hissed. "I need to think," Darby whispered. He sat down on the porch steps before the empty freight office. "This isn't working out at all the way I'd planned."

Dolly found a silk handkerchief. She wet it in the water trough and came over to sit beside him.

"Your poor face," she sniffled, dabbing away the blood. "He was terrible!"

"That he was," Darby said, hearing a sudden commotion and looking up to see Sid and Slick fly through the camel corral to bury their fangs into Mohammed's bony ankles.

The camel squealed in pain. Its head shot down and yellow teeth flashed, but Sid and Slick had expected that and they had already released their bite and had switched their frenzied attack to Mohammed's hind hocks.

Mohammed squealed again. Zack and Bear were yelling and calling their hounds but the hounds were a pair of whirling dervishes as they ducked kicks and narrowly escaped teeth and flying green goo. Their attack continued for several minutes before, to Darby's utter amazement, Mohammed's spirit broke. The huge camel raised his head and cried out in anguish as the hounds gnawed on his hind ankles as if they were soup bones. Mohammed spun awkwardly around and attempted to retreat but Sid and Slick were every bit as relentless in their attack as the Derby Man had been upon the giant a few minutes earlier.

"Get them out of there!" Darby shouted.

After several minutes, Sid and Slick finally came trotting out of the corral of demoralized camels with blood on their fangs and lopsided grins on their faces.

"Well, I'll be damned," Bear exclaimed, grinning broadly. "Ain't them hounds somethin'!"

"Hard to believe," Zack admitted, his chest swelling up with pride. "I always thought Sid and Slick were real special. What do you think, Darby?"

Darby groaned. The thoroughly intimidated and upset camels were screeching and squawking so loudly that Darby could not even think.

What, he wondered, had he gotten himself into now?

Six

THE DERBY MAN sat on the porch and smoked the best cigar that money could buy in Virginia City. It wasn't a Cuban and it wasn't up to his usual standards, but the cigar was decent and he savored it along with half a bottle of French brandy he'd managed to cajole out of a friend who owned the Bucket of Blood Saloon.

Across the yard, he watched Mohammed and the other two-humped monstrosities lying in the dust of their rock-ribbed corral. Every instinct in his corpulent body told the Derby Man to just open the gate and walk away from the camels and cut his losses. The trouble was, he was deep in debt without any great prospects other than writing a dime novel which he was sure he was absolutely incapable of creating. Somehow, then, he would have to find a way to settle the debt owed to the liveryman in Carson City and he'd even have to reimburse Mr. J. Franklin Warner his three hundred dollars.

But how? Darby knew that the Comstock miners, for all the dangers they faced in the hellish bowels of Sun Mountain, boasted the highest hard-rock wages in the world at five dollars a day. But at that rate, given the astronomical Comstock prices for food, drink and shelter, it would take Darby forever to save enough money to pay off six hundred dollars to the liveryman and his New York publisher. Darby shook his head. He refused to work the hellish Comstock mines, where temperatures were well over a hundred degrees and men were often boiled by hidden reservoirs of scaling water or buried in mine cave-ins.

But what else was there for him to do to earn enough money to repay his debts? Perhaps he could snag a job on the *Territorial Enterprise* or even its rival newspaper in Gold Hill. But Darby knew he was not really a journalist. At one time, he'd made lots of money bare knuckles fighting and he was sure he could again with the power he still retained in either fist. But fighting, even under the more humane rules of the Marquis of Queensberry, was a young man's game. Darby had been an undefeated bare knuckles champion in New York, but he knew he would be severely tested by a younger, quicker and scientific boxer who cowardly refused to fight toe to toe.

In his twenties, Darby Buckingham had also been a circus strong man. Just thinking about those days when he'd paraded around the circus grounds in tights flexing his biceps made Darby wince. He was presently too robust to be a circus strong man anymore and besides, that would mean he would have to return to the east coast and Darby was unwilling to make that sacrifice.

What then could a man do who was past his prime, unwilling to labor in the deep, dangerous Comstock mines? Darby would be the first to admit to anyone that he was poorly qualified to prosper in the great American West. He could not ride horses worth beans, could not hit anything with any firearm other than a sawed-off shotgun and had no skill whatsoever with a rope or branding iron. He didn't know a heifer from a hare and tended to get disoriented because he had no sense of direction whatsoever except when the sun was either rising or setting.

"I wouldn't hire me for anything," he said miserably. "And I certainly don't know how I'm going to earn my keep unless I continue to write dime novels or consent to marry some rich female fan—but I love Miss Beavers."

It was awful, Darby concluded, when a person was so limited in his opportunities for gainful employment. Darby knew a lot of men who were wonderfully capable. They could build barns, corrals and cabins, shoe horses, fix guns, brand cattle, rope, ride and do about anything with a high degree of competence. Darby admired such men but admiring them was one thing, being one of them quite another. In his youth, Darby had glorified in his God-given strength and the dynamite in his fists. In middle age, he had been fortunate enough to realize that he also had a gift for storytelling.

Darby sighed. He sipped more brandy and came to his feet knowing that he should walk back up the hill to the hotel where he and Dolly were spending the night, living off J. Franklin's measly advance on his next dime novel.

Mohammed saw him move in the starlight and the immense camel issued an unmistakable warning. Darby looked hard at the gate. He took a few steps toward it and Mohammed suddenly reared to his feet, hissing and squawking.

"Instead of being merciful and turning you loose in this high-desert wasteland," Darby said, "I ought to just bolt the gates and let all of you starve. I'd be doing this country a favor."

In reply, the two-humped Asian camel spat a stream of green goo halfway across the yard but still considerably short of Darby, who snickered with derision. Darby smoked a little longer, trying to decide what he could do to earn enough money to pay his debts and also to live. Unable to come up with any ready answers, he tried to decide what he would do with the camels. One thing for certain, he would never own such filthy, mean-spirited beasts. If they were worth anything but trouble, Bert Jasper wouldn't have been so overjoyed to give them up in repayment for his debts.

Darby walked out to the gate, still hearing Mohammed hissing through his droopy split upper lip like a demented goose. Darby knew, deep down, that he did not have the kind of callous heart that would allow him to simply bar the gate and let the camels starve. However, turning them loose was a real possibility. Darby had learned a few things this day. His friendly saloon owner had seemed to know a great deal about camels, probably because he had befriended the little Arab named Emil. Emil had gotten very drunk and weepy over losing his position as the West's only camel handler. He'd spent a long time telling the other patrons in the Bucket of Blood everything they never wanted to know about camels.

How both the one-humped Arabian camels as well as these two-humped Bactrian camels from Asia had been imported by the United States Army, and how the two-humped Asian camels had proven to be much more adaptable to the harsh western environment. They were slower but stronger beasts than their Arabian cousins, entirely capable of carrying loads of up to one thousand pounds on their humps. Their hair grew quite long in the chill of autumn so that they did not suffer from the freezing Nevada winters as did the Arabians. Furthermore, the two-humpers had much thicker pads on the soles of their feet and did not go lame like their far more tender-footed cousins.

"Who cares?" Darby asked aloud, raising the bottle of brandy and taking a long, satisfying pull. "Let them see if they can propagate running wild in Nevada's high deserts."

Darby was quite sure that, if left alone, Mohammed and his followers really could thrive, even in this arid country. The trouble was, the camels would *not* be left alone. They would be a novelty quickly hunted to extinction. Darby was quite certain that Mohammed and his followers would be annihilated within a month.

"So what do I do with you?" Darby asked, turning around to face the camel corral. "I haven't the heart to starve you to death, nor does my conscience allow me to set you free so that you can all be shot. So, after the hay and my money run out—which at Comstock prices they will very shortly do—what then your fates?"

Mohammed squawked mournfully and the Derby Man, unable to stand the smell of the beasts another minute, turned his back on the camels and slowly trudged up the hill toward his hotel on B Street.

———

THAT NIGHT, Darby slept very fitfully. He kept dreaming of Mohammed. In his dreams, the huge camel was shrieking pitifully as cruel men shot holes in his humps to see if they would leak water instead of blood. It was almost dawn before the dime novelist finally lapsed into a deep, exhausted slumber that lasted until midmorning, when he was awakened by a pounding at his hotel room door.

"Darby, honey?"

Darby ground his palms into his eyes and tasted brandy and too many late-night cigars.

"What do you want, sugarbun?" he called groggily.

"Sugarbun?" Zack cried, guffawing heartily.

"Go away," Darby moaned, covering his head with his pillow.

But Zack, Bear and Dolly would not go away. They kept beating on his door until Darby was forced to struggle out of bed and open it.

"Fer cripsakes!" Zack said. "It's damn near noon. Them camels are so hungry you can hear them howlin' all the way up here!"

"Let them howl," Darby said. "If we opened the gate to their corral, what are the chances we could herd them off somewhere far into the hills?"

"Herd them?" Dolly asked. "Why on earth would you want to do a thing like that?"

While Darby dressed, he explained his question and ended with, "Jasper said they were a curse and I believe him. No one will buy the awful beasts and I can't afford to buy them hay. So, if we could herd them out far enough from the Comstock, they'd at least have some possibility of survival."

"But what about that fortune that Jasper was fixin' to earn with 'em!" Bear demanded. "Have you already forgot about that?"

"Fortune?" Darby asked. "Ha! *mis*-fortune is the only thing that will ever come of those awful beasts."

"That's not so," Dolly argued. "Bear. Zack. Tell him what you learned last night."

Zack was the talker of the pair and he cleared his throat self-importantly. "Thanks to the generosity of your publisher friend, Bear and I were able to buy a few rounds at the bar last night. And the main topic of conversation was your camels."

"They're *not* my camels!"

Zack chose to ignore the outburst. "Guess what, Darby," he said with a sly wink.

Darby finished buttoning his shirt and he walked over to pour a pitcher of water so that he could wash his face. "What?"

"That one fella drinking whiskey with Jasper wasn't entirely lying about the Consolidated Mining Company contract."

Darby turned. "Go on."

The three grinned. It was obvious they had rehearsed this part of the conversation. Zack said, "Why don't you tell him, Miss Beavers?"

"All right, I will. Darby, while you were sleeping this morning, I learned that there really is a lucrative contract that is being drawn up for someone to deliver food, whiskey and all manner of supplies to a godforsaken new mining venture at a place called Gold Peak."

"I never heard of it."

"You will if the ore samples from the Consolidated Mining Company's exploratory shaft prove to be as rich as they're hoping."

Darby frowned. "Why would they want to contract with a man like Bert Jasper and his mangy camels?"

Dolly smiled sweetly. "That's what we need to find out. I suggest that we make some discreet inquiries."

"Discreet inquiries, hell!" Bear swore. "Why don't we all just march over to their head office and find out what kind of money they're offering for delivery?"

Darby splashed water into his face. "Why?" he asked. "Because I don't care what the money is. I have no intention of getting involved with a bunch of camels. None whatsoever— at any price. Under any conditions!"

Zack and Bear exchanged crestfallen looks. Zack said, "But you're deep in debt and that three hundred dollars you got ain't going to last no time at all. And . . . and what about the money you owe to poor Walter down in Carson City?"

Darby steamed. "What concern is that of yours?"

"Well . . . well, we owe a hell of a lot of money up in Lake Tahoe too!"

"Then maybe we *all* ought to strike out for parts unknown," Darby replied, feeling unusually cantankerous.

Dolly came over and used a towel to dry the Derby Man's face. "Your face is as handsome as ever, despite a few little bruises."

"Don't you dare try and flatter me," Darby warned. "I don't want *anything* to do with those camels."

Dolly's voice lost its sweetness. "So what are you going to do with yourself if you won't seize this chance of making a lot of money and you say you can't write any more dime novels?"

Darby's mustache bristled. "I haven't figured it out yet. But I will."

"And what will you do with the camels?"

"They're not mine! I never agreed to take them in lieu of the debt Jasper owes me! I *hate* camels!"

"But everyone on the Comstock considers you to be their new owner."

"I don't give a hoot," Darby said, struggling to keep his temper under control.

Dolly went over and seated herself on the bed. She absently ran her fingers through her golden locks and sighed. "I just never figured you for a quitter, Darby Buckingham."

Her words stung him and Darby reacted with anger. "I've never given up on anything I wanted in my entire life!"

"Oh? You've always wanted to be a writer and you're quitting that. You owe people money and you're talking about quitting the Comstock for parts unknown."

"I wasn't altogether serious," Darby said defensively. "One way or another, a Buckingham *always* pays his debts."

"Fine. Some of the rest of us would like to do the same,"

Dolly said with more steel in her voice than Darby had heard in a long time. "And maybe we've all got a chance at something with this Gold Peak contract. Maybe not. But it seems to us you ought to be willing to at least help us find out."

"Why do I have to do anything?"

"Because, in everyone's mind, *you* own the camels! The Consolidated Mining officials aren't going to be impressed with Zack or Bear or even me. But *you* could impress them and find out how much money could be made in this contract and why they'd even consider camels."

"But . . ."

"If you don't want to do it, fine," Dolly said with a matter-of-fact wave of her hand. "But something has to be done with the camels. And has it occurred to you that this might very well be the opportunity that Bear and Zack have been waiting for all their lives?"

"Not a chance."

"But you don't know that, do you!"

Darby glanced at the two mountain men. He could see hope and pleading in their eyes.

"All right," he said finally. "But here's the deal. If there is a contract and if I can get it with those camels, and if it sounds profitable, then it's yours. You must agree to take complete ownership and responsibility for those camels."

"Aw!" Bear complained. "Fer cripsakes! We don't like them any better than you!"

"Those are my terms," Darby said stubbornly. "If we do this, then the camels are all yours. The very moment you can't stand them any longer, instead of shooting them or turning them loose near a town where they'd be used for target practice, you must both agree to take them at least one hundred miles into the desert and turn them loose where no one can find them. That way, they'll have some chance of survival."

"A hundred miles!"

Darby raised his chin with determination. "That's right. A hundred miles. That's my offer. Take it or I'm packing up and leaving the Comstock on the next stage while I've still got enough money for a ticket for myself and Miss Beavers."

Dolly reacted with anger. "I wouldn't be so confident that you'll have company," she said.

"Dolly!" he exclaimed in an injured voice. "You can't possibly be serious!"

"I am very serious," she insisted. "And remember, because of camels, I almost lost my life."

"And I saved it!"

"True," she admitted, "but I've already thanked you more than once. And now, I think we all need to work together to find out what kind of contract the Consolidated Mining Company is offering and why. Keep in mind that they are one of the richest operations on the Comstock."

Darby felt trapped in something he wanted no part of and he could have bitten off his tongue when he said, "I didn't know that."

"Well, they are," Bear seconded. "And a company like that doesn't get rich by throwing money down an empty mine shaft. We need your help, Darby. We can't get that contract by ourselves. They'd most likely throw us out of their offices."

Darby had to admit it was the truth. Bear and Zack weren't going to impress any mining company executives, and Dolly would impress them, but for all the wrong reasons.

"All right," Darby said. "I'll buy a decent suit of clothes, a new derby and shoes, shirt and tie, then I'll go investigate. But if there is no contract or money to be made, we abandon both the camels and the Comstock."

"And if there is a contract and lots of money?" Dolly asked.

"Then I help Bear and Zack get it before *we* leave the Comstock on the first stage."

"Agreed!" Dolly said brightly.

"Agreed," Bear and Zack echoed, looking very pleased with themselves.

They all shook hands and then the Derby Man ordered a bath and a shave. With his last few dollars he would employ the services of the finest haberdashery in Virginia City. Then he would have a few very candid words with the officials of that prosperous mining company.

In his own mind, Darby was almost certain that this entire issue of a lucrative freighting contract was a clever fabrication created by Bert Jasper to simply confuse the fact that he owed debts he could not pay.

Darby opened his window for some fresh air. The moment he did, he heard the faint, plaintive call of Mohammed and his followers.

Darby reached up to pull the window down tight. But he paused at the last moment. Mohammed sounded hoarse and his squawk was strained and weak.

The Derby Man anxiously chewed on his mustache. Mohammed sounded worried and even a trifle unwell.

Seven

THE HEADQUARTERS of the Consolidated Mining Company were located near the intersection of Union and B streets, next to the ornate brick Storey County Courthouse building. Darby knew that the company had a large mining operation just east of town and an ore refinery in Silver City. When he entered the two-story building, he was immediately impressed by its decor. Three huge crystal chandeliers illuminated the lobby, whose floor was polished Italian marble. Heavy gold-weave draperies adorned the windows and glistening brass rails separated the desks of a small army of silent, scribbling clerks. A very proper old gentleman dressed in a black suit attended and assisted visitors.

"Mr. Buckingham," the man said after introductions, "do you have an appointment with Mr. Poole?"

"No," Darby said, "I'm afraid not. However, I wish to discuss a matter that will be of keen interest to your company's president."

"Which is?" the old gentleman asked politely.

"Which is the matter of your needs at Gold Peak."

"I see." The old man studied Darby very carefully, seemed to make a decision and then nodded. "Would you please take a seat while I announce your presence."

"Of course."

"And whom do you represent, Mr. Buckingham?"

"Camels." Darby had not really meant to say that. It had just popped out of his mouth unbidden.

The old man's eyebrows shot up. "Sir?"

"I represent Bactrian camels," Darby said matter-of-factly.

"Oh. Of course."

Darby took a seat on a shiny walnut bench and folded his arms where he should have been wearing his impressive watch and chain. Blast that suspicious general store owner in Lake Tahoe for the humiliation he'd caused by insisting on keeping the gold watch and chain for collateral!

Fifteen minutes passed before Darby was escorted out of the lobby, through the army of bustling clerks and into the spacious office whose glass door read MR. ALEXANDER B. POOLE, PRESIDENT. As he entered, Darby saw that Poole was a man only in his mid-twenties, of average size and appearance. He wore a thin mustache and a large gold ring on his small finger. Other than that, he was the kind of man that you would not give a second glance.

"A Mr. Buckingham to see you, Alexander," the old gentleman announced.

"Thank you, Father." Poole stood up behind his desk and flashed a wide smile. "Are you *the* Darby Buckingam, lion of the literary world of western dime novels? Is it possible that I have finally met the Derby Man?"

"Then you've heard of me?" Darby said with great modesty.

"Heard of you! Why, I devour your western adventures like chocolate candy! I love them! The last I've been able obtain is *Showdown in Cheyenne*. It was a wonderful story but I wish that you would write more adventures around our Nevada mustangs. We have them running wild in these very hills, you know."

"Is that a fact?"

"Oh yes! Of course, the miners shoot at them and kill the stupid or slow ones, but many are fast and wily enough to run free. Would you like me to show them to you someday?"

"I would very much enjoy that," Darby said, pleased at the way this meeting was starting. The company president's being a fan was going to make Darby's task much easier.

"When?" Poole asked, leaning forward intently. "This afternoon?"

Caught off guard by Alexander Poole's unexpected directness, Darby hemmed and hawed a little. "Uh, well, I have a few complications in my life right now. In fact, one of the reasons I'm here to see you concerns . . . camels."

"Camels? That's what my father said, but I thought he had just misunderstood you. He's getting quite old now, you know. Hearing is one of the many things that fail at an advanced age, including the mind."

"He heard me perfectly," Darby said, irritated that this man should speak in such a way about his father. "In fact, Mr. Poole strikes me as being extremely alert and intelligent."

The younger Poole brushed the compliment aside. "Tell me," he said, "why is a man of your reputation concerned with camels, for heaven's sake? They're horrible beasts. Everyone detests them."

"I know. But to make a long story short . . ."

Poole wasn't interested in hearing about camels. "Darby, can you guess which of your yarns I enjoyed the most?"

"No."

"The one about the Pony Express. I forget its title, but I loved it! You really ought to do more on the Pony Express. What a grand adventure that was! A total financial disaster, of course, but what color!"

"Yes," Darby said, pleased that the man had loved that particular novel. "But about the camels?"

"Oh yes!" Poole leaned back in his office chair and laced his fingers together. "Awful beasts."

"Agreed. But I am told that your company was about to issue a contract to a giant named Bert Jasper who owned the Comstock camels. I understand you were going to employ them on a route to deliver supplies to Gold Peak."

Poole's smile slipped. "That is not public knowledge," he said. "How did you learn about that?"

"From Jasper and his friends. They are not the most discreet of men."

"No," Poole said with a frown. "I suppose not. Anyway, the contract was only in the discussion stage, though we were giving it very serious consideration."

"Were?" Darby asked. "Sir, you employed the past tense."

"Yes. You see, my Board of Directors is very conservative and this entire camel business had them spooked. That, and the unsavory reputation of Mr. Jasper and his . . . his associates. All of it caused us to rethink the issue and we decided not to award Mr. Jasper and his camels the contract."

Darby was not sure if he was pleased or disappointed by this news. It certainly gave him an out with Bear, Dolly and Zack, but on the other hand, he knew how much they were hoping that a way could be found to make some real money off this contract.

"Why?"

"I just told you," Poole said. "We didn't like Jasper or his equally despicable camels."

"But you must have known about him and about the foul disposition of camels from the start. Why then did you even consider the contract?"

A shadow of impatience flashed in Poole's eyes. "Darby, is there some point in this discussion? If not, I'd like to ask you about *Apache Lances*, which I consider your least satisfactory dime novel and . . ."

"There is most definitely a point to my interest in camels," Darby said, "because I have . . . well, reluctantly assumed some proprietary responsibility for those camels."

Poole chuckled. "You can't be serious! What would a gentleman of your standing and fame be doing mucking around with camels?"

Quickly, and leaving out his own miserable financial predicament, Darby explained. He ended by saying, "And so, Mr. Poole, I do feel somewhat responsible for the beasts. And I have two very reputable friends who have asked me to inquire about your camel contract."

Poole frowned. "Well," he said after a moment of deliberation, "there are some problems. First, we have decided to open the contract to all bidders."

Darby sighed. As far as he was concerned, that ended the matter. "In that case, Mr. Poole, we really have nothing more to discuss."

"I'm not so sure," Poole said, quite obviously reluctant to have his famous guest depart so quickly. "In addition to me showing you our mustangs, I'd love to have you over for dinner to meet Mrs. Poole, who also reads every one of your dime novels."

Darby waved his hand in self-depreciation. Now that the camel contract was no longer a matter for consideration and he'd done his part, he was anxious to leave the Comstock on the first stage out of town. "That's very gracious; however . . ."

"And for another thing," Poole said, "there are several cogent reasons why camels might very well be the only solution to our needs down in Gold Peak."

Darby had started to rise in his chair but now he settled back down again. "What do you mean, sir?"

"I mean that our exploratory mine at Gold Peak is nearly inaccessible. The country is so strewn with massive boulders and slashed by deep arroyos that we can't even consider building a freight road directly to the operation for less than a hundred thousand dollars."

Darby clucked his tongue. "That's a lot of money to gamble."

"You bet it is," Poole said. "But we may have hit the jackpot this time. You see, Darby, we employ and grubstake a few old miners year after year. Men like Billy 'Buckwheat' Taylor and Old Charlie 'The Burro.' Legendary prospectors who have—time and time again—found new strikes. A crotchety old fella we had been sending out for eight years without a dime's worth of return to our company is named 'Pokey' Smith. Last year, Smith finally discovered gold at Gold Peak. When we assayed the ore samples he brought back, we nearly went through the roof because they were so rich." Poole shook his head. "Little did we know that Gold Peak is located in the worst country you can imagine."

"So what did you do?"

"We sent men down to sink a shaft and to live as best they could. I haven't been there yet but it's a real hell on earth. No trees, no nothing except rocks and sage."

Darby saw everything with a sudden, blinding clarity. "And the reason you were considering using camels is because there is no hay or water for mules or horses since you can't haul it in on wagons!"

"Exactly! You see, those camels can get along with very little water and they'll chew sagebrush right down to its roots. They'll eat things that a starving goat wouldn't touch. And they're so strong that they can carry huge water bags, just as they have been doing from Tahoe to the Comstock. Camels seemed the only solution until we decide if Gold Peak is rich enough for a major financial investment."

"I see. But why did you change your mind?"

"It was really Bert Jasper," Poole admitted. "Everyone detests the man and he is considered very dangerous and unreliable. Besides that, we were approached by another freighting company. They think they can get wagons within seven or eight miles of Gold Peak and then load mules with water, hay and supplies and deliver them to our new mine."

"That sounds very expensive, Mr. Poole."

"It will be." Poole smiled. "But we are high-stakes players and not adverse to taking risks and investing heavily if the gold and silver deposits are rich enough."

"This 'other' freight company," Darby said. "Did you already issue them the contract?"

"No. There is a great deal of concern whether or not they can fulfill the terms. Our Board of Directors has decided to open the contract to all comers. Any legitimate freighting company will be given some of our least expensive supplies and instructed to deliver them to Gold Peak and return to our stamping mill down in Silver City with a couple of tons of ore. Whoever can complete the terms first and to our satisfaction will be issued an exclusive contract. I expect that they will make a lot of money, Mr. Buckingham. We reward success quite handsomely."

Darby believed the somewhat foppish young man, as Alexander Poole certainly had rewarded himself with a luxurious office.

"Are you and your friends really interested in competing for the contract with camels?" Poole asked bluntly.

Darby cleared his throat. All he had to do was to say no and he was off the hook and off the Comstock. But he wouldn't like himself very much if he did that and he'd have to lie— something that he tried hard to avoid. Furthermore, he was not sure if he could look Zack and Bear in the eye if he had not tried his best to help the destitute former mountain men.

"We might be."

Poole shook his head. "I don't for a minute pretend to understand why someone as rich and famous as yourself would get into something like this unless . . ."

Poole's eyes lit up and he suddenly clapped his hands together with sheer delight. ". . . unless you intended to make it the basis of your next dime novel!"

"What!"

"That's it! You *do* intend to write a western camel story!"

"Don't be ridiculous!"

"Bravo!" Poole cried. "It's all so clear to me now. What a terrific idea! *The Great Camel Race.* I can see that title splashed across the cover right now." Poole closed his eyes; his expression was euphoric.

Darby stormed to his feet. "I have no intention of doing a dime novel about camels!"

Poole's eyes popped open. He smiled and winked conspiratorially. "I understand and I'll respect our little secret. Of course you can't let anyone know the subject of your next western adventure. To do so would be to invite a flood of pretenders to try and write imitations of your story. You and your publisher *must* maintain secrecy up until the very moment that the first copies hit the stands. Isn't that the case?"

Darby did not have the heart to tell this fool how ridiculous an idea it was to pen a novel based on a camel race. Who would be idiotic enough to read it? Those who bought dime novels wanted to read exciting stories of Indians, horses and gunfighters. Of epic struggles pitting brave men and women against the blistering heat of the deserts or the numbing death of the high mountains. No one would buy a story created around a camel race.

"Well, Derby Man, is it a race you want?"

For one of the rare times in his life, Darby found himself at a loss for words.

Poole chuckled happily. "You know something? It might surprise you that I myself have often dreamed of writing a western adventure."

Darby had heard this a hundred times before. Everyone wanted to write, though few were willing to even try. Hardly a week passed in which someone, unwilling to do the tough job of the actual writing, did not approach him with an idea that they wanted to share if he did the hard work and split the proceeds, fifty-fifty.

"How interesting," Darby said, suppressing a yawn.

"Oh, it's exciting all right! And I've laid the groundwork."

"You have?"

"You bet I have! Darby, I've studied the very finest works of all the great literary masters, men like you and Julius Shake-speare."

"Julius Caesar and William Shakespeare," Darby corrected. "The latter wrote a play about the former."

"No matter," Poole said with an absent wag of his mani-cured forefinger. "I've concluded that the masters always use tension, action, romance, color and bloodshed in their novels."

"Bloodshed isn't . . ."

"Believe me, a race to Gold Peak would offer you all those elements and I know that you pride yourself on participating in your own adventures. *That's* why you have lowered yourself to the disgusting level of camels! What other reason could there possibly be?"

"Who would we be competing against?" Darby inquired, struggling to smother his growing annoyance.

"Oh, that depends."

"On what?"

"How we structure the race."

"It wouldn't be a race!"

Poole looked offended. "Well, it would have to be a race, now wouldn't it? Camels against mules, horses, burros, a tribe of Indian runners or whatever. And to make it fair, it would have to be open to anyone with the pluck and daring. The prize would be our lucrative contract."

"Now wait a minute."

But Poole was already lost in his own reverie. He began to babble to himself about what a great dime novel it would be, the Derby Man's finest! Darby Buckingham simply lost all patience with the man. Without bothering to excuse himself, he pushed out of his seat and headed back through the office of busy clerks.

"Mr. Poole," he said to the reserved old gentleman who'd assisted him in the lobby, "you'd better give your son a stiff drink to calm him down or else kick him in the pants and jolt him back to reality. He's on a flight of fantasy."

"Wouldn't be the first time," the old gentleman said with a wink. "I built this company, not Alexander. Now it's all that I can do just to hold it together for my grandchildren."

Darby patted the senior Mr. Poole on the arm. "My sincere condolences, sir."

Eight

WHEN DARBY RETURNED to the hotel, his friends were waiting to hear what he had found out about the Consolidated Mining Company's freight contract. Darby told them what he had learned, omitting only the part about Alexander Poole's wacky idea for a camel race story.

"So the contract is open to all comers?" Bear asked with a look of disgust.

"I'm afraid so."

"Then we're sunk before we're even launched," was Zack's glum pronouncement. "Them contrary camels don't cooperate worth a damn."

"That's for certain," Bear groused. "We might as well turn 'em all loose."

But Dolly wasn't so sure. "Darby, why don't we go find that camel man and hear what he has to say about them?"

"You mean the little Arab?"

"Sure. If that rich mining company felt that camels were the only alternative to their freighting problem, perhaps we don't really appreciate their abilities."

"There's nothing to appreciate about the ugly things," Zack grumbled. "They ain't as fast as a horse and they're so mean and cantankerous they won't behave."

"They won't behave for *us*," Dolly corrected, "but they might behave for the camel man."

"I don't know," Darby said. "I think we ought to just forget this whole thing and leave the Comstock before we look like complete fools. I do have some kind of reputation I'd like to uphold."

"Of course you do, darling. But winning that rich Gold Peak contract would be a wonderful feather in your cap. Another western adventure that you could even write a dime novel about."

"Now don't *you* start that."

Dolly linked her arm through Darby's and smiled. "You look so handsome in your new shirt, suit, tie and derby. Let's go find the camel man and see if he might even help us win the contract."

Darby grated his teeth in exasperation. He didn't want to win the contract—not with camels.

"The little weasel's name is Emil El Babba," Zack said. "Easy enough to spot because he wears a turban, a flowing gown so dirty you could stand it up by itself, sandals and a long, curved sword stuffed through a sash around his waist."

"My, my," Dolly said cheerfully. "At least he sounds colorful. We shouldn't have a bit of trouble finding Mr. Emil."

"I can hardly wait," Darby said as Dolly pulled him out of his room.

THEY SEARCHED all over Virginia City and finally found Emil where they should have looked in the first place. He was happily feeding the famished camels the last few bales of hay in the yard. When he saw Darby and his friends, Emil tossed his pitchfork aside and yanked out his long curved saber.

"You!" he screeched, revealing that he was missing his front teeth. "You *starve* my pretty babies!"

"What's he talking about?" Bear asked.

"The camels, I think," Zack replied.

"Of course he is," Darby said as he measured the scrawny little Arab and saw that the man was prepared to use that saber even against guns.

"We came down to feed them," Darby said, only half telling the truth. "And I can see that we are almost out of hay. I'll buy some more."

"The finest!" Emil shouted.

"Yes," Darby said, "the finest. How many bales do we need?"

"A hundred!"

"No problem," Darby said, not at all sure if he had enough money left to buy so much hay. "But after that, I'm afraid that the camels are going to have to live off the land—so to speak —until they earn their keep."

Emil jammed his saber back through his belt into its scabbard. The thing was so long it came almost to his ankles. Darby saw an old Arabian blunderbuss nearby which he was sure that Emil El Babba would also have died attempting to use.

"We want to ask you some camel questions," Darby said.

Dolly smiled and her eyelashes fluttered. "Emil, we know that you're the only *real* camel expert in the entire West."

Emil liked that. His bare, bony chest swelled up. He grinned toothlessly and bowed low. He was a most interesting figure, Darby thought. Short, wiry and wild-looking but also a little fierce and unpredictable. One had the idea, looking at Emil El Babba, that he might weigh no more than one hundred pounds soaking wet, but he was a fighting rooster, one you'd have to kill before he would surrender anything he thought important. The Arab had deep-set eyes, bushy eyebrows and a long, droopy mustache. His loose, colorful garments were rags. He wore no shoes but there were seven rings on his toes. He was a most unusual man.

Darby walked over to the porch and sat down to wait until the Arab had finished pitching hay to the camels.

"Notice," Dolly said, "that they don't spit on Emil or try to kick or bite him."

Darby held his own council. He offered cigars to Zack and Bear, who accepted, and they all smoked contentedly while Emil disappeared in the pen. A few minutes later, he appeared with a bowl in his hands.

"What do you suppose he's got?" Bear whispered.

The question was answered immediately when Emil raised

the bowl and poured about half a gallon of camel milk down his gullet. The Arab smacked his lips and wiped them with the flowing garment that covered his arms. He walked over to his blunderbuss, took his time checking the load, then came swaggering back across the yard to confront Darby.

"You own Mohammed and all the beautiful camels now?"

"Mr. Jasper thinks he can get out of his debts by giving them to me, but . . ."

"If you feed, you own," Emil decreed. He then squatted cross-legged in the dust and cradled the old Arabian blunderbuss across his lap. "What we do now, boss?"

Zack tittered at that. "He called you 'boss'! What do you say about that, Darby! Looks like he expected all along to come to work for whoever took ownership of the camels. Looks like he's been weaned on camel milk!"

Bear chortled but Dolly failed to see much humor and told him to hush. "Anyone who can love such ugly creatures deserves my respect."

"Ugly?" Emil shook his head with vigor. "Not so, beautiful princess."

At the "beautiful princess" line, Dolly tittered like a schoolgirl while the Arab continued. "You see ugliness, I see beautiful camel. Notice how large and beautiful the eyes."

"They do have pretty brown eyes," Darby admitted.

"They are more than beautiful, sir," Emil said, his enunciation very pronounced and easy to understand. "Camel's long, lovely eyelashes provide the eye with shade from the sun. When a desert storm blows, the camel's eyelashes go together like fingers."

To demonstrate his point, Emil laced his fingers together and grinned with his gums. "And then," he continued, "the beautiful camel's nostrils close so it does not choke like you and me, eh, boss?"

"I see," Darby said. "The humps, do they hold water for times of emergency?"

Emil giggled. "Oh no, boss! The humps are fat!"

"Fat?"

"Yes, boss! You can tell how well a camel has been fed by the humps. If they are hungry and not fed enough, like these poor camels, then the humps very small and the camel looks very, very bad."

"If the humps do not hold water, how does he live so long without it on the desert?"

The Arab raised his hands, palms up and outward. "This I cannot say," Emil answered. "But he drinks very, very much. Sometimes, if camel is too thirsty, it drinks too much and will die. Like a horse eats too much grain and die. Eh?"

"Uh-huh."

"Camel very strong. Stronger than ten mules!"

"Oh bull!" Zack growled.

"Okay," Emil conceded, "two or three mules. But still very strong. Eat anything. Leather shoes, sticks, rocks. Anything. He work very hard but cost you very little, boss."

"Can you control them?" Dolly asked. "Make them behave?"

"Oh sure, beautiful lady. I control. Camels love Emil El Babba."

"If that's true," Darby challenged, "where were you when Mohammed scared our team of horses witless and sent us plunging off the mountain road on the way to Lake Tahoe!"

Emil El Babba shrugged. "No understand, boss."

"These camels! They almost got us killed."

"Beautiful camels very, very nice."

"The hell you say! They are very, very bad!" Zack said angrily. "And if you can't keep them under control, I'll sic Slick and Sid on them. Understand?"

As if on cue, the pair of hounds, who were tied to a hitch rail, began to snarl and raise their hackles. In response, Emil jumped to his feet, tore his saber out of its scabbard and waved it at the hounds. This caused both Bear and Zack to draw their Bowie knives.

If Darby hadn't stepped in right away, there would have been a terrible fight. Emil would have been killed, of course, but he probably would have gotten in a few serious licks at the mountain men before he'd succumbed to their knives.

"All right! All right!" Darby yelled. "Zack. Bear. Put those knives away."

"Him first with that sword," Bear hissed.

"All of you put your weapons away right now!"

The three obeyed the Derby Man's orders but there was a lot of glowering going on and it was obvious that the mountain men and the Arab weren't going to ever be friends.

"Listen," Darby said, taking Zack and Bear aside and keeping his voice low so that he could not be overheard, "you two old goats *need* Emil! Without his help, you haven't a chance of winning the Consolidated Mining Company's rich contract. Don't you understand that?"

"Yeah, but . . ."

"There's no 'buts' about it! If anything happens to Emil El Babba, we might as well open the gates and turn the camels loose because it's hopeless."

Zack and Bear could see the logic of this. Bear said, "All right. We won't touch the little camel boy until we learn his tricks. But after that when we don't need him anymore, he's either heading for the hills or we'll carve him up like a Christmas turkey."

Darby could see that it was useless to attempt to reason with the angry mountain men. "Why don't you both take your hounds and hike back up to the saloons and have a few beers?"

"With what?" Zack demanded. "We're broke as a pair of Paiutes."

"Here," Darby said, digging a ten-dollar bill out of his wallet. "Stay away from the fast women and bad whiskey. Behave yourselves and try to discover exactly who you will be competing against for that contract."

"You'll be competing against 'em too, won't you?"

When Darby did not reply, Dolly said, "You can't run out on us now! Not after what you said about Mr. Poole being such a fan. Why, if you were to leave without joining the race, he'd probably be so angry he'd award it to our competitors."

"I don't want any part of this," Darby said firmly. "How many times do I have to make that clear?"

"But Emil won't listen to us!" Dolly argued. "To him, you're the boss. If you quit this race, we'll be finished."

"Does that mean that you wouldn't come with me if I wanted to leave tomorrow?" Darby asked the woman he loved.

Dolly bit her lower lip. "I'm afraid so, darling. As much as I love you, we have debts and responsibilities. And I think, if Emil can handle those awful camels, that we also have a very good chance of winning us a rich mining contract."

Darby sighed. He studied Dolly's lovely face, then those of his friends and finally Emil. "Can these camels work very hard on little food or water?"

"Sure, boss! Beautiful camels work very hard for you."

"All right," Darby said finally. "Let's find out exactly what we have to do to win this contract."

"Whoopee!" Bear shouted as Zack did a little jig around the snarling hounds.

"But once it's won," Darby said quickly, "it needs to be understood that Dolly and I are leaving the Comstock Lode. We want no part of this miserable camel business, no matter how rich that contract."

Bear and Zack nodded with reluctant agreement.

"Come on," Dolly urged with a smile, "don't sound so threatening. We're all in this thing together and that is exactly as it should be."

"Maybe," Darby grumped, "but I'd feel a lot happier if we were in this without those camels."

Emil El Babba overheard the Derby Man and he shook his head, looking very unhappy. "Boss *must* be good to beautiful camels."

"Or what? They'll spit on me again?"

"Maybe so," Emil confessed. "But beautiful camels no like to be talked bad to. Very sensitive, boss."

Darby groaned. "I'm sure they don't understand a word I'm saying about them."

"Camels can tell by voice if they are loved. Make *big* difference in how hard they work."

Darby didn't believe a word of it. "Come on," he said to Dolly. "Let's go back up to town and see what we can find out about that contract."

"You buy finest hay. One hundred bales!" Emil called after them. "Camels very hungry. Hungry camels no work. Get very mean, boss. Bite. Spit. Do everything bad. Worse than American children."

Darby didn't respond. He still didn't know where he was going to come up with enough money for that much hay. Fifty bales might satisfy the little tyrant.

Maybe Emil could not count. Darby scowled. Emil was ragged and pushy, but he was no fool. Darby had a feeling that dealing with the Arab was going to be every bit as difficult as dealing with that herd of stinking Bactrian camels.

Nine

YOUNG ALEXANDER POOLE paraded into the crowded assembly hall fifteen minutes later than promised and raised his manicured hands in a dramatic appeal for silence. "Gentlemen! Gentlemen! Please. Sit down and hold your questions until after I've outlined the terms of the Gold Peak contest!"

Darby puffed rapidly on his cigar, vastly annoyed. He was not a man who appreciated waiting for anyone. Also, he did not appreciate the boisterous behavior of the rowdies that filled the hall.

"Now," Poole said when the unruly crowd had quieted. "I can tell you in all sincerity that the Consolidated Mining Company is as excited as any of you about this race to Gold Peak and back to the Comstock. We've the interest of newspaper reporters from the *Territorial Enterprise* as well as the *Gold Hill Daily News* and the *Reno Evening Gazette*. We've even received word that several California newspapers are sending reporters!"

At this bit of news, the audience erupted in boos and shouts of derision. One tall freighter with a bushy beard and a face the color and texture of redwood bark shouted, "Ain't none of us give a damn about your publicity, Mr. Poole! What we want to know is when we can get this race started and how much the contract is going to pay the winner!"

"Yeah!" another man echoed, followed by another and another. "Quit horsin' around and get to the bones of the matter!"

Poole flushed with anger. "I'm not horsing around! The

Consolidated Mining Company is prepared to start the race the day after tomorrow. The terms are very simple. Each contestant will be given five hundred pounds of supplies to deliver to our men at Gold Peak. If he delivers them, he will be guaranteed fifty dollars no matter when he returns."

The crowd nodded. That sounded fair.

"The return trip will require each contestant to transport five tons of crushed ore to our stamping mill in Silver City. The first one to deliver wins the contract. It's worth a thousand dollars and requires just one round trip a month delivering supplies and returning with Gold Peak ore."

"For a thousand dollars a month, I'd deliver to Denver and back!" a man shouted from the rear of the room.

Everyone laughed. Poole chuckled but then his demeanor turned quite serious as he said, "Round trip delivery to Denver, gentlemen, might be easier than a run to Gold Peak."

"Aw, come on!" a man shouted. "Gold Peak is in Nevada, ain't it?"

"Yes," Poole admitted, "but it's also near Death Valley and I am warning you that there are very few water holes when you get down in that bad desert country. Furthermore, our exploratory mining crew has had several skirmishes with the Paiute Indians. Nothing major, but they'll steal you blind and even break open your water barrels so that your stock will die of thirst. They want to butcher any dead or crippled animals left behind."

At this news, the faces of the men in the assembly hall darkened. One man yelled, "Why don't the United States Army do something about them renegade Indians? That's what our taxes are payin' 'em to do, ain't it?"

"The Army is spread thinner than whitewash and you know it," Poole said. "They can't and they won't deploy troops way out in the desert just to protect the interests of a private mining concern. Furthermore, these Indians seem more inclined to harass rather than attack—providing we are vigilant and well armed."

"If I get one in the sights of my Hawken," Zack bellowed,

jamming his big buffalo rifle overhead and pumping it up and down, "then you can bet they's harassed their last!"

The roomful of frontiersmen burst into laughter. These were rough-and-ready fellows accustomed to hardship and danger. Every man among them knew the general location of Gold Peak, knew that it rested in country plagued by brain-boiling heat, no water and pesky Paiute Indians. They also knew that the promised contract and resulting profits were commensurate with the risks they'd have to take with their wagons, men and animals.

"Exactly how far is it from here?"

"Two hundred miles." Poole stroked the waxed tips of his mustache, then flicked dust from his custom-tailored coat.

"Ha!" a freighter shouted. "Maybe it's two hundred miles as the crow flies but it sure as hell ain't the way we'll have to travel."

"It's two hundred miles each way," Poole repeated, "but I admit that the road is poor. Fact is, the road is worse than poor—it's awful. There are places where it's washed out and there are long stretches of soft sand where wagons can sink to the axles. The road peters out entirely about six or seven miles short of Gold Peak."

This was not well received. The freighters shouted their displeasure and it was several minutes before Poole could re-store order to the room.

"Gentlemen! Please! If this were an easy run, the Consolidated Mining Company wouldn't be offering a thousand dollars a month just to deliver a few hundred pounds of supplies and return with five tons of ore. The entire run is just four hundred miles long, once a month. Now, any of you that can't see a big profit in that are in the wrong business."

"What about the bonus prize we heard was going to be offered to the contract winner!" someone demanded.

"Oh yes," Poole said with a tolerant grin. "Well, I wasn't going to let the cat out of the bag, so to speak, but the winner will be a main character in a western dime novel written by none other than Mr. Darby Buckingham—better known to readers around the world as the Derby Man!"

Darby groaned and clenched his fists. "I *never* agreed to that!"

"Aw," Poole called, "what's the harm in admitting that you intend to use this race as the basis for your next bestselling dime novel!"

The roomful of men shouted and applauded. When order was finally restored, Poole held up his hands for silence. "When Mr. Buckingham first came into my office inquiring about the contract, I couldn't imagine why a man of his fame and fortune would be asking about Gold Peak. But then, when I learned he had purchased the Comstock camels . . ."

Hoots of laughter and ridicule drowned out whatever Poole was saying next. Darby, enraged by the foolish pronouncement he had just heard, felt he had to leave the assembly hall or else he'd grab Poole by the throat and throttle the pompous imbecile.

"Where are you going?" Dolly cried, grabbing his arm.

"Outside for some fresh air," Darby groused through a smoking cigar clenched between his teeth. "Find out what we need to know and tell me about it later."

Outside, Darby hurled his cigar to the dirt. "That blasted fool!" he raged, grinding his cigar to pulp under his heel.

"Are you speaking about my son, Mr. Buckingham?"

Darby turned to see Mr. Arthur Poole. At the sight of the old gentleman, Darby regretted his outburst but not his sentiments. "Yes sir, I'm afraid that I am. You see, I have no intention of writing about camels and this insane race to win your company's contract."

"What a shame," Poole said, clucking his tongue. "I think it would make a mighty fine story. Quite unusual."

"Oh, it would be that."

"Of course," Poole said, "I can understand why a man of your age and condition would decline such a challenge."

"What?"

"After all," the old man said, ignoring the look of outrage

on Darby's face, "it will be a dangerous run. My son didn't come right out and say so, but we've lost several men and a number of livestock to the Paiutes and the desert heat. It's hellish country down that way. Certainly no country for men like us who are long past their primes. Eh?"

"Speak for yourself, sir!" Darby snapped. "I'm in top-notch shape."

Poole smiled with tolerance. "Of course you are," he said without a hint of sincerity. "And I'm sure that that beautiful woman that you seem so fond of will do just fine without your presence."

"Who said I wasn't going?" Darby challenged.

Poole's silver eyebrows arched. "Well, sir, it's obvious enough that you are not supportive of this venture. Although I confess I am surprised you would allow such a beautiful woman as Miss Beavers to attempt such a harrowing journey without your constant protection."

Darby suddenly realized he was being played like a fiddle. He shook his head and chuckled. "You, sir, are are a crafty old fox. But why then is your son so obtuse?"

"Oh, Alexander is plenty bright enough," the old man said, amused rather than angered by Darby's unflattering description. "Alexander just lacks maturity. You see, he was born and raised under rather sheltered circumstances and he never had to rely on his own wits."

"That much is quite obvious."

"Mr. Buckingham," the old man said, "I don't need to have my only child's shortcomings thrown in my face. I'm already painfully aware of them. Which brings me to the point of this conversation."

Darby had been about to add something else about Alexander's insensitivity and arrogance, but now he held his tongue and listened.

"The point of this conversation is that I want *you* to be responsible for the safety of Alexander during the run to Gold Peak and back."

"What!"

Arthur slipped his arm through Darby's and led him off to where they could speak without being overheard. "Alexander doesn't know this yet, but I intend to see that he goes along on this great adventure."

"But why?"

"Isn't it obvious? He's my only child and—well, I confess that he is hopelessly spoiled. Alexander grew up in the East and attended an Ivy League college. He's always had everything but . . ."

"But now," Darby said, "you compare him against other men his age and find that young Alexander is much too full of himself."

"Exactly. I am a self-made man, as you are, Mr. Buckingham. And while I have worked all my life so that I could give Alexander the finest start possible, I can see now that he's missed something very important. That something is adversity. Life has been far too easy for Alexander."

"And you want to throw him into the bowels of hell in one fell swoop?" Darby shook his head. "I think it's unfair to Alexander to expect him to either accept what you have in mind or even survive it."

The old man's brow furrowed. "I am convinced you are wrong, Mr. Buckingham. I believe most fervently that this is the opportunity I have long sought to teach Alexander about humility, resourcefulness, the ability to reach down inside and display the kind of grit and fortitude that characterizes the brave miners we employ."

"I don't know," Darby said. "If he were my son, I'd . . ."

"You'd do the same thing in a moment. But you'd want a strong, resolute fighter that you could trust to lend aid and assistance if your son really got into a desperate fix."

Arthur Poole placed his liver-spotted hand on Darby's broad shoulder. "*You*, sir, are that man."

"If I remember correctly, you have a daughter-in-law."

"That is correct."

"What does she think about this test of fire?"

Arthur's eyes misted with pain. "Mr. Buckingham, I know

that you will never betray what I am going to tell you now. My lovely daughter-in-law says that if my son doesn't grow up and stop thinking only of himself, she will leave him and take my grandchildren back to Boston."

A wave of pity assailed the Derby Man, yet his better judgment still advised him to avoid taking on such a huge responsibility. His feelings must have shown on his face because the old man said, "Please!"

"But how . . ."

"That's my problem, not yours. I will insist that Alexander go along in the capacity of a . . . a referee or overseer to make sure that no skulduggery occurs."

"He won't survive," Darby announced without a moment's equivocation. "Not if the trail to Gold Peak is as treacherous as he told those men in the hall."

"Mr. Buckingham," Arthur said, "the trail to Gold Peak is much more dangerous than my son told the audience. And now that we are entering the searing heat of summer, the hardships will be multiplied ten times over what they were when we set up the exploratory mine shaft in the relative cool of this past winter."

"Mr. Poole," Darby said, "I'll already have my hands full with those blasted camels and taking care of Miss Beavers. I just don't feel that I can handle anything more."

The old man looked into the Derby Man's eyes for a long moment, then his thin shoulders sagged with defeat. "I'm really sorry to hear that, Mr. Buckingham, because if you had agreed to look after my son, I would have helped your two old friends become quite wealthy."

Poole turned and walked away but Darby, after a moment's reflection, spun around and went after the man. "Listen," he said, "if for some reason Alexander were seriously injured or killed, I . . ."

"Then it would be tragic but not your fault. As you well know, Mr. Buckingham, this world offers no guarantees. Not even that we enjoy the precious gift of life one hour from now."

Darby hadn't the heart to refuse this fine old gentleman any longer. "No matter what happens, if I give my word that I will do my best to help your son, to protect him from any and all dangers, then you must promise that Bear and Zack receive your most profitable freighting contract."

Arthur Poole's face lit up. He stuck his thin, soft hand out and said, "Agreed, Mr. Buckingham!"

"And," Darby added before shaking, "if I am killed, that you will see that Miss Beavers is also taken care of for as long as she lives."

Arthur hesitated. "In what manner do you have in mind?"

"A hotel," Darby said, remembering that the first time he had met Dolly she had owned and operated the Antelope Hotel in Wyoming. "She can run a successful hotel."

The old man pursed his lips and nodded slightly. "By chance, I happen to own a fine little hotel down in Gold Hill that is not, at present, being well managed. If Miss Beavers is really qualified, she could have that position as long as she wishes."

Arthur frowned. His hand was still extended but Darby hadn't yet taken it. "Anything else?"

Darby didn't want to push his luck but he was certain that this rich mining magnate would promise him anything in the desperate hope he could transform his son. "Yes, one thing."

"What?"

"A hundred bales of hay for my camels as well as whatever grain and provisions we will need to win this damned race."

"Do you really think you can win?"

"Why not?"

Arthur grinned. "Yes, Mr. Buckingham, why not indeed!"

Now Darby finally took the old man's hand in his own and squeezed it firmly. "Then we have a deal!"

TRUE TO ARTHUR'S PROMISE, the hay was delivered to Darby's camels that very same afternoon. As dusk fell across the Comstock Lode, Darby and Dolly strolled down to visit Emil El Babba and the camels.

"Camels very happy now, boss."

"Good! We'll be leaving for Gold Peak the day after to-morrow, bright and early."

Emil frowned. "What," Darby asked, "is wrong now?"

"Camels pretty thin. Need to eat for a week or two, boss."

"I'm afraid that just isn't possible. The race begins the day after tomorrow."

"But boss, camels not ready! Little humps mean little fat. Camels skinny now and very weak."

"They don't look a bit weak to me," Darby said. "And we need to win this race or 'boss' will turn beautiful camels loose in the desert and bad men will fill them full of holes."

Emil paled and his hand flew to his mouth. A stricken look came to his eyes and he appeared so upset that Darby immediately regretted his words.

"Listen," Darby said, "I'll hire a wagon to drag along lots of hay and barrels of water for the camels until the road peters out."

Emil was very much relieved. So relieved that he wanted to show and tell Darby and Dolly all sorts of things about his camels.

"These are camel saddles," he explained, taking them into the little office that Bert Jasper had vacated.

"They're funny-looking," Dolly giggled.

"Camels like. Put load between the humps like so."

Emil demonstrated how the supplies would be attached to the strange-looking camel packs.

"But . . . oh, never mind," Dolly said.

"What is it?" Darby asked. "If you don't understand something, then ask."

"Will we take along ladders?"

"Ladders? Why in the world would we do that?"

"How else could we possibly get up so high to mount them?" Dolly asked.

Emil's black eyes crossed and then snapped back into focus before he said, "Beautiful camels lie down to be loaded and mounted, beautiful lady."

"Oh, I get it!"

Darby looked away for a moment, then cleared his throat. "Any other questions, darling?"

"Not that I can think of."

"Good. Emil, everyone that intends to enter this race has been asked to show up tomorrow at noon and collect the supplies they are supposed to deliver to Gold Peak. I think I'll pick them up with the hay and water wagon that I will rent for this trip. That way, we won't need to spook anyone else's livestock."

"Good idea, boss."

Darby started to turn but suddenly something hit him in the back, right between the shoulder blades. It felt like a sparrow had crashed blindly into his body.

"Oh, Darby!" Dolly exclaimed, making a face. "Mohammed got you again!"

Darby yanked off his suitcoat and his face mottled with rage. There was a thick wad of green goo and half-digested hay stuck to his new coat.

Mohammed's head was hanging over the top rail of his corral and he began to squawk triumphantly.

Darby took a menacing step toward the camel. It drew its lips back from its teeth and spat again, narrowly missing this time.

Darby's hand flashed to the derringer he carried in his coat pocket but Dolly grabbed his arm. "No, don't do it!" she pleaded. "He didn't mean to spit on you."

"Didn't mean to? Ha! Of course he meant it!"

Darby tried to wrestle Dolly aside but when he finally managed to do so, there was Emil El Babba with his sword drawn. The sword was pointed straight up but there was little doubt from Emil's expression that he was prepared to stop anyone, even the boss, in order to save Mohammed.

Darby's voice shook with fury. "You had better tell that fleabag camel that he can thank me for his hay and his life. And tell him that he had better stop spitting on me or I'll . . . I'll barbecue him!"

Emil made a horrible face. "I speak to Mohammed, boss. I explain. Boss no hurt beautiful camel. Emil fix."

"Well then, do it!" Darby roared, before he shook the disgusting wad from his new coat.

"Come along," Dolly said, forcing cheer into her voice as she took his arm. "It's time for dinner."

Darby grumbled and rumbled all the way back up to C Street. And once more, he asked himself how he had ever been so foolish as to get himself involved with such despicable beasts.

Ten

DARBY HADN'T EXPECTED anything approaching the size of the immense crowd of revelers that thronged the street in front of the Comstock Mining Company headquarters. Gamblers strolled arm in arm with prostitutes, children scurried about playing tag while stray dogs strutted, sniffed and sometimes fought. Darby saw many newspaper reporters with their little yellow pads, interviewing rough freighters and spectators alike. Two fiddlers and a banjo player were picking a lively tune as another of their party danced with hat in hand to catch both cash and coin.

There were dozens of freight wagons lining B Street surrounded by the restless crowd. Each represented an entrant in the race to Gold Peak and all were impatient to receive their five hundred pounds of supplies and then race south.

Bert Jasper, his ugly face still badly misshapen by Darby's fists, sat perched high atop one of the freight wagons. When he looked down and saw Dolly and the Derby Man, he growled, "You'll never reach Gold Peak alive! Not with those camels and not against me and the boys!"

Dolly clutched at Darby's sleeve. "My gosh, *he's* in the race too!"

"It doesn't surprise me," Darby snapped. "A winner-takes-all race is bound to attract misfits and cutthroats."

Dolly turned her face away from the giant's leering eyes. "How many outfits are we racing against?"

"I have no idea, but I'm sure we'll find out in the next few minutes."

To Darby's surprise, Arthur Poole, rather than his pompous young son Alexander, emerged from the mining headquarters. With assistants on either arm, Arthur was helped up onto the bed of a buckboard. He raised his hands for silence. In a few minutes the crowd settled down to listen.

Arthur had a sheet of paper in his fists. He surveyed the street full of contestants and spectators, cleared his voice, then said in a voice that carried surprisingly well, "Ladies and gentlemen, this race will begin one hour after the last contestant has received his shipment of supplies for our employees in Gold Peak. After I am finished, drive your wagons around to the back of our office and get them loaded."

"How many of us are in this?" Jasper shouted.

Arthur held up the sheet with a list of names. "There are ten freighting companies entered. We rejected several other hastily formed operations knowing that they were totally unprepared to face the trials they will face in the days and weeks ahead."

"What about those gawddamn Comstock camels?" another rough-hewn freighter demanded. "Mr. Poole, you know that our stock won't tolerate those stinking beasts."

Arthur pinned the man with his pale blue eyes and said, "Sir, the Comstock camels are entered and will compete on an equal footing with mules, oxen and horses. If that does not meet your approval—or anyone else's—you may withdraw from your entry right now with my blessings."

This announcement was extremely unpopular and caused an undercurrent of resentment to flow through the other contestants. Several of the freighters shot hard glances in Darby's direction and others muttered thinly veiled threats. Bert Jasper just leered malevolently.

"We aren't very popular, are we?" Dolly whispered.

"No," Darby said, "that's why I insisted that Bear, Zack and their trouble-making hounds remain with the camels. We'd better assume that our camels will be shot if the opportunity presents itself to these men."

"Maybe we shouldn't do this," Dolly said. "I mean, we can

still back out. We don't have to drive this wagon around behind the office and collect those supplies."

Darby wanted to explain that he had shaken hands in an
agreement made with Arthur Poole to watch and protect Alexander. To a Buckingham, a handshake was as good as a
bond. Darby still had no idea in what capacity Arthur's foolish
son was going to travel with them, but that was not his problem.

"And so," the old man was saying as he raised a shaky fist
overhead, "in behalf of the Comstock Mining Company, I
want to wish every contestant the very best of luck. Watch
your backs and keep your water barrels safe. Remember, it's
fifty dollars for delivery, and the first outfit that returns with
five tons of ore wins our freight contract. Any more questions?"

There were none, so Arthur again wished them good luck,
then added, "And by the way, you all know my son, Mr.
Alexander Poole. He will be traveling independent of everyone but always watchful. Any skulduggery whatsoever among
you will result in an immediate disqualification. Alexander
will be the sole arbitrator of all disputes."

The freighters grumbled and one called, "We can take care
of our own problems, Mr. Poole. Don't need no overseers or
referees!"

"I'm afraid I disagree," the old man said. "And if you cannot accept Alexander's role, then I strongly suggest, Mr.
Cravens, that you withdraw from this contest."

Cravens blushed with anger. "I'll stick," he snorted. "But I
won't tolerate no nosin' around my outfit by anyone—not
even your fancy-pantsed boy."

The elder Poole didn't appreciate that insulting reply.
Darby could see that the old man had to really struggle to
keep from disqualifying Cravens on the spot.

After clearing his throat, Arthur said, "Mr. Cravens ex-
cepted, I hope that the rest of you will invite my son to join
you for supper or breakfast. Remember, he's in charge of the

Comstock Mining Company and he has my complete confidence and backing."

There were a few more instructions and Darby glanced aside to see Alexander, his wife and two children. The young man stood beside a fine palomino and a burro loaded with what Darby supposed were basically the same supplies that his company would send out with their prospectors, men like "Pokey" Smith, the old fellow who had made the strike at Gold Peak.

Darby frowned as he watched the young mining company president. It was clear that Alexander did not want to leave his lovely family, but equally clear that his wife was trying to boost his spirits and make him climb onto the palomino.

Alexander's cowardly demeanor disgusted the Derby Man and caused him to mutter, "What a spineless whelp!"

"What, dear?" Dolly asked, turning to follow Darby's gaze. "Who is that handsome young man?"

"That's Mr. Poole's son, Alexander."

"What a nice family. Why would that handsome young man be so foolish as to ride out alone to Gold Peak?"

"You heard his father. They need someone to oversee the event and make sure that there is no 'skulduggery.' "

"Why couldn't they have just sent one of their best employees? After all, it's clear that poor Alexander doesn't want to leave his family. Why, look at him!"

Darby groaned. Alexander was . . . dear Lord, he was *weeping* as he hugged his children! Darby had to turn his head and he prayed that Arthur did not notice his son's pitiful behavior.

"How tragic," Dolly said, sniffling. "This is awful!"

"Brace yourself," Darby growled, "because it's going to get a lot worse before it gets better."

"Whatever do you mean?"

"Never mind."

"Excuse me. Mr. Buckingham? Mr. Darby Buckingham?"

Darby glanced down from the wagon, which Dolly was driving. "Yes?"

"Jim Frank from *Gold Hill News*. What did you think about those remarks these other drivers made concerning your camels?"

"Sounds like they don't like them," Darby deadpanned.

"*Nobody* likes them," Frank said. "Are you expecting treachery?"

"Yes," Darby admitted as the reporter scribbled away on his yellow pad.

"And if that is the case, Mr. Buckingham, do you really think it is safe to take a woman along?"

"That's for me to decide, Mr. Frank!" Dolly said angrily. "Besides, I'm taking *him* along!"

Frank scribbled that down as he talked. "Is that really the case, Mr. Buckingham?"

"So it would seem."

"Do you think, if the other contestants do not shoot your camels, that they can really transport five tons of ore back to Silver City?"

"I do. We have a dozen camels, each capable of carrying seven or eight hundred pounds."

"But they'll also have to carry you, as well as Miss Beavers and the others. And don't forget food and water."

Darby watched as Jasper spat a wad of chewing tobacco that landed on the back of one of their horses. The giant laughed like the bray of a mule. He clutched a rifle loosely pointed in Darby's direction, leaving no doubt as to his challenge or intentions to seek revenge on the trail to Gold Peak.

Following Darby's hot eyes up to the terrible face of Jasper, the reporter swallowed nervously, then said, "Would I be correct in guessing that that huge, ugly fellow was not exactly an admirer of your dime novels, Mr. Buckingham?"

"I'd be amazed if he could even read," Darby said. "Dolly, let's get out of here."

But Frank was not finished, and the street was so jammed with pedestrians and wagons that Dolly couldn't yet move their team forward. Frank leaned closer. "Mr. Buckingham, I was inside the hall when it was announced that you were undertaking this adventure in order to use it as fodder for your next novel rather than to win the contract. Is that true?"

"Of course it isn't!" Dolly said, clearly upset by the inference. "Darby is the kind of man who plays to win—always!"

The reporter's pencil raced. "Is that correct, Mr. Buckingham?"

"Yes."

"Then you really are going to try and win?"

"Correct."

"With camels?"

"With camels and with my friends, Zack Woolsey, Bear Timberly and my fiancée, Miss Beavers. It's going to take all of us pulling together to have any chance of being the first to deliver five tons of ore back to Silver City."

"Will you pen the adventure while you are on the way down to Gold Peak and back, or wait until you return?"

"I don't know," Darby heard himself say. "I'll probably take notes during the race. However, my retentive powers are quite extraordinary and . . ."

"Oh, Darby! I'm so happy you've decided to write again!"

Frank stopped scribbling. He stared at Darby. "You mean you actually considered retiring?"

"Well . . ."

Frank's pencil scratched furiously across his notepad.

"Wait! Don't print that," Darby said.

"But it's big news. I'm sure that it will be picked up in the East, where your yarns enjoy such enormous popularity."

"They're not 'yarns,' sir! They are novels."

"Dime novels. No offense, Mr. Buckingham, but they are hardly classic prose."

Darby's fist shot out. He grabbed the startled young man by the shirtfront and, one-handed, hoisted him completely off his feet to struggle in mid-air.

"Darby!" Dolly shouted. "What's the matter with you? Let go of Mr. Frank this very instant!"

Darby hurled the reporter away and the man skidded on his

behind underneath a horse that jumped and nearly trampled him.

"What is wrong with you!" Dolly exclaimed as she reined their team after the procession of contestants slowly beginning to work their way around the block to pick up supplies.

Darby immediately felt ashamed of himself. "I'm a little preoccupied and irritable right now."

"Don't worry. We'll win and, even if we don't, it's not a matter of life or death."

"You're right," Darby conceded. He did not want to tell her that, judging from what he'd seen and heard from the other freighters, it *was* a matter of life or death. For all of them, including young Alexander and the Comstock camels.

Darby could not explain how he could sense the hatred and hostility he felt from the other freighters. And Bert Jasper and his cutthroats were just waiting for the opportunity to get their revenge.

"Cheer up," Dolly said. "We're going to make this a race they'll long remember on the Comstock. And after we win it, Bear and Zack will get rich."

"And what will we do?" Darby asked, managing a smile.

"How about we go back up to Lake Tahoe and take up housekeeping at their cabin while you write this story?"

Darby chuckled. He slipped his powerful arm around Dolly's tiny waist and hugged her.

"You're starting to look forward to this adventure, aren't you?" Dolly said.

"Not really."

"Oh sure you are! Come on, admit it!"

But at just that moment, Darby had a glimpse of young Alexander Poole, whose wife was practically hoisting him onto his pretty palomino.

"Let's go," Darby growled, "before I get sick to my stomach."

"Poor dear!" Dolly said. "I didn't realize that you had an upset stomach."

Darby didn't bother to explain.

Eleven

DARBY, BEAR AND ZACK had finished loading hay and barrels of water when the sound of gunfire floated down to them from above.

"That'll be the start of the race," Zack grunted, heaving a box of food and cooking utensils into the back of the wagon. "I think we'd best get started before we get left too far behind."

But Darby shook his head. "With our camels, we don't dare become a part of that stampede. We'll wait another hour until the road is clear and then we'll quietly head south."

"Darby," Zack fretted, "it sure galls me to start out dead last."

"We've already gone over this," Darby said patiently. "God Himself couldn't keep those freighters from shooting our camels if we tried to join the race."

"Yeah, I know, but being last means that all the water holes farther south will have already been sucked up or polluted."

"That's why we have camels and water barrels," Darby argued.

Even as he said this, they saw the other nine contestants come bursting out of the middle of Virginia City to race headlong down the street toward Six Mile Canyon. Almost all of the teams were pulled by mules rather than horses, for it was generally believed that they could handle the intense heat better on less feed and water. But there were teams of horses and even a team of men afoot leading a long string of Mexican burros.

Darby saw that Bert Jasper and his thugs were in the lead but were being pressed hard as they shot into the narrow mouth of the canyon, taking the entry curve on two wheels.

"Damn fools will kill themselves and their mules before they reach Fort Churchill," Bear muttered.

"Darby?" Dolly twisted a blond ringlet around and around her index finger. "Maybe we should get started right now and try to at least keep them in sight."

Darby had been afraid of this waffling and last-minute change of heart. "Listen," he said patiently. "We have a plan. We all know that we can't keep up with the others over the first hundred miles. But after we reach desert we hope that things will be different. That's when the advantage will switch to our camels."

"But if we're too far behind," Zack argued, "then we'll never catch up."

"Sure we will," Darby said. "Remember, the road ends about six or seven miles this side of Gold Peak. That's when all the others will have to unload their wagons and pack the supplies on horses, burros and mules. We'll already have our supplies on these camels."

"Yeah," Bear said. "And even more important, our camels will be able to carry the five tons of ore out by themselves while everyone else will have to pack it all the way back out to their wagons."

"Exactly," Darby said. "So we will take the lead at Gold Peak and, hopefully, never look back on our way to Silver City."

"It's just that I hate to crawl out of here like a pack of turtles," Bear grumped as he watched the last team of competitors disappear down the canyon. "That looks like a lot more fun than herding those stinking camels."

"Yeah," Zack lamented.

"Be patient," Darby assured them. "We'll get started soon. Besides, Emil El Babba hasn't gotten the camels saddled yet."

"What the hell is he waiting for?" Bear demanded.

"He says he wants them to finish their last supper."

"Well, the hell with that!" Zack snapped. "Let's get going!"

Emil heard this outburst. Stiff-backed, he set about preparing to get Mohammed while Darby and the others remained far out of spitting range and watched. They were all surprised when the Arab reappeared from a barn with a buggy whip. Entering the corral, Emil quickly cornered Mohammed and, after dodging a few kicks and bites, the Arab whipped the big camel's legs until it bawled and cowered in a corner. Emil twisted a rope around the beast's lower jaw back where it had no teeth.

Mohammed wasn't pleased to be singled out and he spat at Emil but the Arab ducked and whacked Mohammed across the underside of his gaunt belly. The camel squealed, lips quivering like those of a petulant but naughty child.

"I thought Emil and that camel were in love," Zack drawled as Mohammed's ears flattened against his knobby head.

"Love," Darby observed, "doesn't change the fact that camels are miserable creatures."

"Look!" Dolly cried.

They all watched as Emil smacked Mohammed's front knees. The huge camel dropped first his front and then his back end to the dust. Mohammed kept squawling his displeasure while, only a few yards away, Sid and Slick barked and wagged their long, thin tails, thoroughly enjoying the show.

Once the camel was down, Emil wasted no time in getting a saddle cinched and lashed to its humps. The pack saddle consisted of four long, heavy poles laced together and padded with leather. Emil's hands flew as he tied a blanket neatly over the leather base of the saddle.

Then, to Darby's horror, Emil turned and called, "He's ready, boss!"

"Oh no! I'm riding in the wagon!"

But Emil just laughed. "Boss *must* ride finest camel."

"Not a chance!"

"Aw, go on!" Bear urged with a malicious glint in his eye.

"We all can't ride in the wagon and the boss should ride the biggest, nastiest camel."

"Shut up!"

"Chicken?"

Darby squared his shoulders. "All right," he said. "But if I ride Mohammed today, *you* have to ride him tomorrow. Agreed?"

Bear's grin sagged. "I'd rather die than be seen on one of those two-humped sons'abitches."

"That can be arranged too," Darby gritted between clenched teeth.

It took all of his courage to march over to the huge, squawling beast. Even lying down, it was a real struggle to get a leg over the camel's back and hop on board. "What now?" Darby gulped.

Emil raised his hands into the air before the camel. "Up, Mohammed!"

"Whoa!" Darby yelled, grabbing anything and everything when the monster lifted its back end first, nearly pitching Darby over its head.

"Hang on!" Zack yelled, as he and Bear doubled up with laughter.

Darby clung to Mohammed as the beast threw its front legs out, snorting and bawling, then began to rise higher and higher until Darby felt like a squirrel atop a towering pine tree.

"My heavens!" he shouted, aghast at the height he had achieved and the rolling sensation of the camel as it shifted its flat feet adjusting to Darby's weight. "God help me!"

"That looks like fun," Dolly said, leaving the others and coming over to stand beside Emil. "I think I'd like to try that. I've already ridden in more than my share of wagons."

Dolly, knowing what to expect after watching Darby and riding a smaller and more agreeable camel, mounted quite easily. In a few minutes, she was giggling and swaying on top of a second camel.

"Hey! This *is* fun!"

"Fun?" Zack muttered. "I once talked to a private in the United States Cavalry that had to ride one of those so-called 'ships of the desert.' He said they call 'em that because a camel's back rolls like a ship in heavy seas. He got seasick every time he had to ride one and he said it was pure hell going out on camel patrol."

"Best we stick to the wagon," Bear said, and resumed loading supplies.

When they left a short time later, Zack and Bear led off driving their hay, water and supply wagon. Next came Emil, who, to Darby's immense relief, led Mohammed by the rope. With Dolly in second camel position, the other camels fell in behind, all of them vocal in their displeasure to be traveling.

As he swayed down Six Mile Canyon leaving the Comstock Lode behind, Darby wondered what kind of mess he had gotten himself into. And somewhere up ahead, Alexander Poole was riding around thinking he was the boss when everyone knew he was a frightened fool. A mere poppycock that strutted about his father's empire and grand office having never accomplished an honest day's work in his entire life. Darby prayed that no harm would come to the young banker before he and the Comstock camels overtook their competitors. After that, who could say what might happen?

They followed the shallow, meandering Carson River and camped that evening a few miles east of Fort Churchill. The camels, irritable and hungry, had to be beaten away from the hay on the wagon because Darby wanted them to eat the grass or the leaves on the cottonwood trees. Later, when there was nothing but sage and sand, the camels could devour the precious bales of hay.

That evening, Emil tried to show them how to make the camels drop to their knees to be mounted or loaded. During this lesson, Mohammed nipped Darby so severely on the upper arm that it bled and the Derby Man ground his teeth in a black rage. He would ride this miserable beast into the ground and he would do it without a shred of mercy.

In the morning, an army patrol came riding out to investi-

gate but when their horses caught wind of the camels they
went crazy and refused to come closer despite being severely
punished. Finally, Darby heard the sergeant in charge yell,
"Patrol dismount!"

The men dismounted and, a few minutes later, the sergeant
and a peach-faced young corporal came marching into their
camp.

"Good morning," Darby said.

"It was until our mounts caught wind of these damned
camels!"

Darby's smile faded. "Sorry."

"What are a woman, an eastern dude, two old men and an
Arab doing out here with camels?" the sergeant demanded
after sizing up things.

Darby did not appreciate the soldier's descriptions or tone
of voice. "What is your name, Sergeant?"

"Regan. And this is Corporal Taylor."

"I see. Well, soldiers, this is a free country and we are on
our way to Gold Peak. How far ahead are the wagoneers?"

"A bunch passed late yesterday afternoon. They warned my
commanding officer you'd be coming along."

Regan shook his head with disgust. He was a large man
with an underslung jaw and a face burned red by sun and too
much bad whiskey.

"You are the sorriest outfit I've *ever* seen."

Darby took a step closer to the man and placed his hand on
Regan's shoulder. The move caught the sergeant by surprise
and he pulled back, but the Derby Man's fingers bit into the
muscle of his shoulder.

Regan snarled and doubled up his fists. "Let go of me or
I'll drive my hand into that belly of yours up to me wrist!"

"Try it, bub! Try it and I'll break you like a limb from one
of these trees."

Regan tried to bat Darby's hand from his shoulder but
Darby only increased the pressure and the Irishman shrank
with pain. "Let go of me!"

Darby released his grip. "Unless you have some reason for

coming out to visit our camp, Sergeant, I suggest that you and your corporal leave at once."

Regan's left shoulder drooped lower than his right but he was trying not to let on how much pain he'd just suffered.

"And I suggest," Regan said, backing away with clenched fists, "that you and your traveling freak show had better not count on the United States Army to pull your fat out of the fire."

Darby took several steps toward the sergeant but then, when Regan whirled and stomped off toward his patrol, the Derby Man reined in his anger.

"You should've killed him for that kind of talk," Zack said.

"And then we'd not only have to worry about nine different freight companies, but also the United States Army," Darby said with annoyance. "Emil!"

"Yes, boss!"

"Let's get these camels loaded up and on the road. Time is wasting."

For the next forty minutes, they all worked to hitch up the team, reload supplies and get the camels saddled and packed. It wasn't quick or easy but the camels seemed to cooperate a little better than they had on the Comstock.

"Emil," Darby said when they were finally ready to go, "I expect us to have these camels packed and ready in one half hour tomorrow morning."

"One half hour?"

"Yes. We seem to be forgetting that we are in a race."

"Emil no forget."

"Well," Darby said, realizing he was wrong to misdirect his anger from the sergeant to the more convenient Arab, "then let's go."

When they left the shade of the spreading cottonwood trees along the Carson River, Bear told them that, other than the Walker River, which they'd cross the next day, they should not expect any more free running water or trees for shade.

"After the Walker," Bear warned, "it's going to be damned hot and damned dry."

"With camels, that's supposed to be to our advantage. We'll do fine," Darby called back from the flagship of his tall camel. "Just fine!"

But he knew that was just talk. As far as Darby could see in every direction from his lofty vantage point, there was nothing but barren sage-covered hills and rocks. Years before Darby had ridden south toward Death Valley. It had been the summertime then, just as now. He still remembered a heat so intense that he burned his lungs with each searing breath. And always there was the fear of losing your water, or not finding more water.

Down in this desert country, tiny mistakes proved fatal.

Twelve

THE NEXT DAY was hot and dry. Darby soon learned that the Bactrian camels were cantankerous, plodding beasts of burden. There were other species of camels bred for speed and endurance called "dromedaries" and they were the favorites of the bedouins in the Sahara Desert. Emil claimed that a good riding dromedary could average five miles an hour and cover fifty miles a day. Darby's Comstock camels, on the other hand, were fortunate to go half that fast or far no matter how relentlessly they were pushed.

Zack and Bear were tearing their hair out over the agonizingly slow pace of the camels. It took them ten long hours to reach the Walker River; horses could cover the same distance in half that time.

"At this rate, it'll only take us about two years to reach Gold Peak," Zack said sarcastically.

"You forget that we'll make much better time than our competitors when the road gets sandy and impassable for wagons," Darby again reminded his friends.

"When that happens, what are we going to do with our hay, water barrels and supplies?"

"Load them on the camels, of course."

"Bales of hay?" Bear asked with disbelief.

"Sure," Darby said, "I'll bet that, with Emil's guidance, we can tie everything left in the wagon onto those camel saddles."

Bear and Zack looked appalled. The two mountain men were unusually quiet that evening as everyone sat around the campfire listening to the chomping and grinding of the camels' teeth as they mowed through the sagebrush as if it were sweet clover.

"They'll eat anything, won't they?" Bear growled with disgust.

Later that evening, Darby and Dolly walked hand in hand out beyond the fire and stood to gaze up at the starry heavens.

"Look!" Dolly whispered. "A shooting star!"

"I missed it," Darby said, "but there will be others."

"Of course there will. Did you know that a shooting star brings you good luck?"

"No."

"Well, it's true. Tomorrow," Dolly said, "I should have good luck."

Darby searched the heavens for another shooting star but he didn't find one. When you thought about it, that was the way of life. Good luck—like shooting stars—came only when you were least expecting it and rarely when most desperately needed.

"What are you thinking about?" Darby asked.

Dolly was slow to answer. "My son and daughter. I was thinking that, after all these years, how nice it is to know that I can finally write or visit them whenever I want."

Darby could understand that. He'd helped Dolly to find her long-lost children and he knew it was a real comfort to her to be freed of mistakes from her past.

"Darby?"

"What?"

"When we get married, I'd like to have children again."

Darby had been about to light a cigar, but now it slipped from his hand and fell to his feet. "We're too old for that now!"

"No we're not! Besides, think how wonderful they'd be with your brains and my face and figure."

"If it was a boy," Darby said peevishly, "he could do worse than to look like me."

"Why, he couldn't do better! But I know you'd have liked to have been a little taller."

"I'm just fine," Darby said. "And I don't want any children."

Dolly kissed his mouth. "I think I might be able to change your mind about that, given time."

"Don't count on that, my dear," Darby said with a grin.

They lapsed into an easy silence for a few more minutes before Darby finally saw a shooting star. Actually, they both saw it together.

"Now," Dolly said, hugging his arm, "we're *both* going to be lucky."

"We can use all the luck we can get."

On their way back to the campfire, Mohammed raised his ugly head and made an unusual hissing sound. Darby reached into his pocket for his derringer but Dolly stopped him and said, "Just ignore him."

"I'd like nothing better," Darby said. "But I won't be spat upon again."

"That derringer of yours isn't big enough to drop something the size of a camel anyway," Dolly said, pulling Darby along toward the camp.

"Then I'll get Bear or Zack's buffalo rifle," Darby vowed. "Or even ask them to shoot that miserable beast."

"I'm sorry to hear you feel that way," Dolly said. "I'd thought, after two days of riding Mohammed, you and your camel might have finally come to terms."

Darby scoffed. "He hates me and I hate him. Those are our terms and they'll not change until one of us breathes our very last."

This sentiment was hardened the next morning when Mohammed kicked Darby in the seat of the pants so hard that he lifted the Derby Man completely over a clump of sage.

"That ties it!" Darby raged. He yanked his pistol out, took aim and fired.

His bullet missed badly and before Darby could reload,

Emil El Babba was grabbing the derringer and sinking his teeth into Darby's wrist.

"Owww!"

Darby dropped the little pistol and the Arab scooped it up and hurled it far out into the Walker River.

"Now you've done it!" Darby raged, balling his fists.

Emil drew his saber. "Emil does not wish to cut off boss's beautiful head!"

"Try it and I'll bend that sword around your neck so that you can shave every morning without a razor!"

They might have killed each other right there and then—to Bear and Zack's great amusement—if Dolly had not thrown herself between them.

"Stop it, both of you!" she cried. "Is this any way to start out hoping to win a rich freighting contract? Emil, without Darby these camels will be turned loose and they'll be shot. Darby, without Emil we're just wasting our time."

Darby turned on the camel and Mohammed bared his long yellow teeth at him, split lip fluttering aggressively.

"I've had it with that one!" Darby shouted. "If I'm forced to come near him I'll go for his throat with a knife, I swear I will."

"Want me to turn Sid and Slick on him?" Zack asked hopefully.

The two hounds riding in the wagon had been quiet. But now, at the mention of their names, they began to get excited. Darby, remembering how they had punished and completely cowed Mohammed by gnawing on his hocks, was sorely tempted to turn the dogs loose.

The Arab seemed to read his mind. "Emil kill dogs!"

"Oh yeah!" Zack hissed, drawing his Bowie knife. "We'll see about that!"

"Stop it!" Dolly screamed. "Stop it this minute or we are all turning back right now."

Zack and Bear wanted to win the Comstock Mining Company contract so badly that they swallowed their pride. Zack sheathed his knife and marched away, yelling at the hounds to be quiet or he'd put a boot to both of them.

"When this is over," Bear said to the fierce little Arab, "there will be a day of reckoning."

Emil spat on the ground in defiance.

"You're like a bunch of five-year-old boys!" Dolly cried with exasperation.

"Emil," Darby ordered in a gruff voice, "saddle me a different camel to ride. If you're so fond of Mohammed, then *you* ride him."

"Yes, boss."

Darby stomped off to make busywork. He was angry and thought that in his entire life he had never hated anything so much as camels. Especially Mohammed, though they were all disasters.

Ten minutes later, Bear and Zack had their team hitched and the wagon loaded. As they marched around, they occasionally threw hard looks at Emil, who stuck out his tongue. Dolly appeared disgusted and Darby just wanted to get moving.

All that morning they followed the Walker River down to Walker Lake. It wasn't much of a lake, really. Almost treeless, and the water had a disagreeable alkaline taste that the camels didn't seem to mind.

"Emil?"

"Yes, boss?"

"If you can get those camels to drink their absolute maximum fill, do it. It might be a long time before we find another source of water."

Emil nodded. Taking Mohammed's jaw rope, he led the animal out into the shallow waters of the lake. The other camels followed. They stood knee-deep in water squawking and gawking. Mohammed decided to relieve himself and most of the other camels did likewise, which sent Zack and Bear into spasms of laughter.

"You shut up!" Emil cried, hand on the hilt of his saber.

Zack and Bear laughed even harder.

"Stop it!" Dolly commanded.

She looked so angry that Bear and Zack turned away, red-faced. Dolly called out to the little Arab, "Perhaps if you moved them on down a little farther they might still drink."

Emil led Mohammed through the shallow water until they were about a hundred yards south. After ten or fifteen minutes, Mohammed lowered his head and drank. And drank. And drank!

Darby did not know how much water the camel swallowed, but it must have been a lot because Mohammed probably gulped a hundred times. The other eleven camels filled up as well.

"That's great!" Darby called. "That might hold them all the way to Gold Peak! Nice going, Emil!"

The Arab swelled up with pride. He looked especially pleased and relieved because he had clearly been dejected since their angry confrontation along the Walker River.

"Take a bath!" Zack shouted.

Emil's smile died and Darby twisted around to confront the old mountain man. "You smell a little gamey yourself. Why don't *you* take a bath?"

"Why don't you try and make me?"

Darby threw himself at Zack, whom he outweighed and easily outmuscled. He grabbed the tall, thin man by the arm and flung him headlong into the lake. Bear tackled Darby from behind and they went rolling and wrestling into the water. Bear was still a hell of a handful and when Zack joined him, Darby would have been outmatched if Dolly had not jumped headlong into the fray.

In moments, it was a free-for-all, with each of them taking turns dunking and being dunked. Dolly proved herself to be quite a tussler and was right in the thick of it until Darby surged to his feet, with Bear on his back, shouting, "Enough! Enough!"

Everyone was ready to quit. Emil was laughing and that got them to laughing, and pretty quickly the camels were squawking and the dogs barking.

When they left Walker Lake a short time later, all hostility and ill feeling between them had been washed away clean. Darby's suit was ruined and so was his new derby hat, but he didn't care and pulled the sopping thing down hard over his forehead. He looked at his friends, then at Emil, and he winked at the Arab. Emil winked back and Dolly, her dress plastered to her voluptuous body, appeared more luscious than the Derby Man had ever remembered.

Darby believed the shooting star's luck had given them their free-for-all in Walker Lake. Now they were a team. Even Emil and his crotchety camels. Darby could sense a dramatic change. For the first time he thought that they might actually make it down to Gold Peak and back without killing each other.

BEAR AND ZACK led them along the treeless eastern shore of the long, shallow desert lake. By mid-afternoon, they were in the desert, following the wagon ruts of their competitors.

That night, they made camp in the sage. Darby opened a water barrel. They filled their canteens and Dolly's cooking pot, then they watered the horses from smaller buckets. When the horses had their fill, Bear and Zack carefully poured the remaining water back into the barrels and re-placed them in the wagon before covering them with a tarp.

They arose early the next morning and Darby caught and saddled his own camel, one with deceptively mild brown eyes. It hissed and tried to bite him, but following the lessons he'd learned by watching Emil, Darby was able to whack the camel into resentful submission. Not only did he saddle his camel, but he also felt confident enough to help Dolly saddle hers. This made Emil's job much easier and reduced their departure time considerably.

Emil continued to lead Mohammed by the rope tied around his lower jaw. When Darby protested, arguing that the Arab should conserve his strength and ride the huge camel, Emil only smiled and shook his head.

"Emil very strong," the Arab explained, walking steadily to the south.

Darby guessed that the Arab really was strong in spite of his lack of height or muscle. Darby was five times more powerful than Emil, but he could not possibly have walked through this hot country, mile after scorching mile, like Emil El Babba. Physical strength, Darby realized, was not always measured in terms of muscle, but also in terms of stamina.

Even Bear and Zack had to admire Emil after a few more days on the trail.

"He's leaner and tougher than a coyote," Bear said grudgingly.

"Quicker than a jackrabbit too, I'll bet," Zack added. "I saw him round those damn camels up this morning. I never knew someone that skinny could run so fast or walk so long."

"Me neither, but I can't for the life of me understand why anyone would walk when they could ride."

"It's his way," Darby said. "Just like mountain men, he's developed his own ways of doing things over the years and he's not about to change them now."

"He's a strange one," Bear said.

"I don't trust him," Zack said.

Darby wasn't sure he trusted Emil either, but he knew that, along with the others, he had certainly come to respect the Arab. Just before dusk, when the weary camels were beginning to squawk and get particularly ornery, they saw something unusual silhouetted on the southern horizon.

"What is it?" Dolly asked.

"I don't know," Zack said.

"Wagons," Emil told them, shading his keen eyes. "Many wagons."

Darby frowned. "Which way are they moving?"

"Not moving."

"Then they must be camped," Zack said.

But Emil shook his head and his brow furrowed deeply. When questioned, he would say nothing, yet from the concern in his brown eyes, Darby had the feeling that something was very, very wrong.

"Shall we push on to meet up with them? Or," Darby asked, "shall we make camp?"

"Camels very, very tired, boss. No travel after dark."

"All right," Darby said, not wanting to fight the beasts after such a long, hard day.

"We'll probably meet them tomorrow."

Everyone looked to Emil, whose eyes were locked on the distant specks that he said were wagons. They half expected him to say more but the Arab's dark, serious face was a mask. He walked away shaking his head in troubled silence.

Thirteen

THAT NIGHT, the coyotes howled so long and so loud that Sid and Slick chewed through each other's collars and went out to fight. The fight must have been a terrible one because it awoke the entire camp. Then, just before dawn, the two hounds came streaking back with about twenty coyotes hot on their heels. The howling dogs and snarling coyotes spooked the camels and horses and everything took off running.

"Grab the horses!" Darby shouted, jumping up and pulling on his shoes. "Emil, the camels!"

In the dim, predawn light, Darby could see that everything was in chaos. Horses were rearing back on their picket line and camels were scattering like prairie dogs under the wing of a hawk. Darby understood as clearly as the rest of them that if the horses escaped they would have nothing to pull their wagon.

Sid and Slick shot under the picket line with the coyotes gnawing the tips of their tails, and the horses went crazy. They broke their picket line and went racing off toward the Comstock Lode. Zack and Bear cussed up a storm and chased the horses a few hundred yards but that only made them gallop faster.

The only good news was that the first pale fingerlings of daylight revealed that the camels had not gone very far because Emil always hobbled and belled Mohammed, from whom the others would not stray. But now the huge camel was bawling and hopping around, trying desperately to buck and run despite the hobbles. Before Emil could calm the beast, it tripped over a clump of sage and crashed into a pile of rocks. While Mohammed lay momentarily stunned, Emil managed to loop his jaw rope on the big animal and get it under control.

Hawken rifles crashed like twin cannons and the last of the coyotes shot off into the brush. The badly torn hounds were so grateful for their worthless lives that they buried their heads under their paws and quietly endured a blistering string of cuss words from their irate owners.

Zack came over to join Darby, who stood watching the last of their horses disappear on the southern horizon. "Well, Buckingham, what the hell are we going to do with our wagon?"

"I'm not sure."

"Will camels pull wagons?"

"I don't think so. Ask Emil."

"You ask him," Zack snapped in anger.

Darby went over to Dolly, who was ministering to the bloody hounds. The Derby Man squatted on his heels, placed a hand on Dolly's shoulder and said, "Are they going to live?"

"Yes, but the poor babies were eaten half alive."

As if confirming Dolly's opinion, Sid and Slick began to whimper and feebly wag their thin tails. Darby was not overly sympathetic. He recalled how these dogs had thoroughly intimidated the old man up at Lake Tahoe, then had savagely attacked and defeated Mohammed. Besides, they had been the ones who'd gone after the coyotes, not the other way around.

"Maybe," Darby said, "it will teach them humility and good sense. A little fear in their black hearts wouldn't hurt, either."

"You're so cruel sometimes," Dolly sighed, using a wet handkerchief to wipe blood from Sid's torn ear.

Darby didn't appreciate being called "cruel" but this was no time to voice his objection. They were in a fix, thanks to the damned hounds, and he needed to know if they had any options. He went over to the Arab, who was removing Mohammed's hobbles. "Will camels pull wagons?"

"Not these camels and not that wagon, boss," Emil said, his expression and manner uncharacteristically blunt and angry.

"That's what I thought. Then I see no help for it but to unload the wagon onto the camels and keep going. We had planned to do it anyway but I was hoping to hold off until we neared Gold Peak."

Darby studied Mohammed's hocks. They were rope-burned from his attempt to break the hobbles. The big camel's shoulder also had been opened up when he'd tumbled over the sage and a pile of rocks.

"Is he going to be fit to travel?"

"Camel very brave and strong!" Emil's eyes darted to the hounds and suddenly hatred flared like the flame of a torch. "I kill goddamn Sid and Slick!" he cried, hand reaching for his saber.

"Darby!" Dolly shrieked, reading murder in the Arab's eyes.

"Emil! Stop!" Darby commanded, trying to grab the Arab, who easily sidestepped him and rushed at the dogs.

At the sound of Dolly's cry, Zack and Bear turned to see the onrushing Arab. Both mountain men lunged for their rifles.

Darby tackled Emil from behind and tore the saber from his hands. "There will be no more trouble, Emil."

"Hounds must die!"

"I admit they deserve to die, but, without a wagon to ride, it's Zack and Bear who will suffer. They'll punish the hounds, not you."

"Emil, please," Dolly begged, shielding the dogs. "Sid and Slick went after coyotes. They didn't mean that Mohammed should be hurt."

Emil thought about this for several moments before he dipped his pointed chin, then stomped past Bear and Zack, hissing, "You hate camels, I hate hounds! Ha!"

Bear took a threatening step after the Arab. "Why, you little . . ."

"Enough!" Darby shouted. "It's time to get these camels packed."

The two mountain men loathed the animals and it was well into the morning before they finally managed to get all their water barrels, supplies and the unwieldy bales of hay lashed to their humps. By then, both mountain men had received multiple kicks and bites.

"All right," Darby said, forcing his camel to its knees and mounting the beast, "let's saddle up and ride!"

Zack and Bear threw themselves onto the backs of their camels and when the animals surged to their feet, both men struggled frantically in order to keep from taking a tall tumble. With Emil now leading a limping Mohammed, they continued south. After a quarter mile, Bear became violently ill from motion sickness and Zack turned ghostly white.

"It feels odd at first," Dolly shouted back to the nauseous pair. "That's because a camel swings both left then both right feet forward together at the same time. You'll get used to it after a few days."

The mountain men were breathing deeply and chose not to respond.

"Something is wrong up ahead," Darby said as they grew nearer to the wagons they'd spotted the evening before.

Suddenly, a man came staggering out from under the wagons. He was clutching his stomach and appeared to be either gut-shot or violently ill. He tried to yell and wave his arms but instead collapsed and was rendered helpless by a series of violent dry heaves.

"The poor man!" Dolly cried, urging her camel forward.

"Help!" the man croaked. "Help!"

Emil put Mohammed to his knees and leaped from the big camel. Darby was not far behind. As he rushed forward he saw dead men and dead mules scattered everywhere.

"What happened?" Darby cried, kneeling beside the retching man.

"Poisoned us," the man gasped. "Someone put poison in the . . . the water!"

"Can't we do something for him?" Dolly wailed, racing up to fall beside the man and cradle his head in her lap.

The man's eyes fluttered open and he gazed up at Dolly. His skin was mottled gray and his breathing labored. He continued to retch but there was nothing in his stomach and he had become so exhausted that each spasm became progressively weaker.

"We've got some castor oil," Zack said. "And some whiskey."

A flicker of hope shimmered into the dying man's eyes. "Whiskey? Oh, please! My boots for a bottle!"

Zack hurried off and returned with a bottle which he quickly uncorked. "Here, fella," he said, tipping the man's head and pouring the whiskey into his open mouth.

After emptying the bottle, the man retched no more. Instead, his body relaxed and he grew very quiet. He sweated profusely and his eyes wandered around the sky, unfocused.

"Who did it?" Darby asked. "Who poisoned the water?"

"Dunno."

"Was it Bert Jasper?"

The dying man rolled his head back and forth. "Don't think so. Jasper way up ahead."

"Then who was with you when you camped last evening?"

The man tried to speak, but another series of spasms doubled him up. Then he threw his eyes around at the faces above, belched whiskey fumes and sighed his last.

"He's dead!" Dolly exclaimed, tears springing to her eyes. "The poor man has been poisoned to death!"

Darby walked over to the wagons, where he found a barrel of water. He stuck a finger into it and brought it to his lips.

"Well?" Bear asked, coming up behind him.

"I don't taste anything," Darby said. "You try."

"Not me," Bear said, shaking his head and taking a hurried backstep. "If they didn't taste it, I won't taste it. Could be just a drop will kill you, Buckingham."

"I don't believe that," Darby said, grimly surveying the

death camp. He counted five poisoned men and seventeen mules and horses.

"Whoever did this is sure a cold-blooded killer," Bear said.

"He is that," Darby replied. He wondered which of the freighting teams would have committed such a heinous act.

"What are we going to do with them?" Zack asked, glancing up at the hot, rising sun.

"Bury them."

It took Darby only a few minutes to find some shovels that had been intended to dig wagons out of soft sand. The burying of the men, however, took nearly two hours because the ground was hard and rocky.

All the while, the sun rose higher and hotter. Sid and Slick, smelling death and feeling the pain of their awful coyote whipping, howled piteously. Somewhere far out in the sage, coyotes howled back in victory. Darby had always thought that coyotes only howled at night. Now he knew different.

It was noon before they left the wagons, fresh graves and poisoned livestock, which drew clouds of buzzards overhead. With the stench of death thick in their nostrils, the camels rolled their great brown eyes like agates and kept up a constant squawking.

"Let's go," Darby said, wiping sweat from his brow and confiscating a sawed-off shotgun and a box of shotgun shells from one of the wagons. He used ten rounds to shatter the poisoned water barrels so that not even a complete fool would come upon them and take a lethal drink.

Satisfied that they could do no more in this place of death, the Derby Man forced his camel to the ground, mounted and was ready to leave. Following the wagon tracks of those going on before him was easy. Finding out who had managed to sneak poison into the poor unfortunates' water barrel was going to be far more difficult.

Sid and Slick suffered a great deal that day, for they had become accustomed to riding in the wagon and sleeping all afternoon. At least now, Darby thought, the sorry hounds would be so tired by night that they would be content to remain in camp and lick their wounds.

Late that afternoon, they came upon another group camped down in a dry arroyo. They would have missed the camp except for a flume of black, oily smoke that drifted up from a fire made of creosote bush.

"Leave the camels up here while I go down and have a word with them," Darby ordered the Arab.

"Yes, boss."

Before Darby could leave to hike down into the arroyo, Dolly hurried to his side. "I'm going with you."

Darby balanced his shotgun in his fists. He did not expect that this group would try to kill him unless it belonged to Bert Jasper.

"We're coming too," Zack said as he and Bear arrived with their rifles.

Darby had no objections, so the four of them crept up to the edge of the arroyo and peered down at the camp.

"Does anyone recognize them?" Darby whispered.

"I saw them in Virginia City," Bear said. "I remember that big, pigeon-toed fella with the red checkered shirt. He heads one of the outfits."

"You know his name?"

"Fowler. Abe Fowler."

Darby stood up in plain sight and hailed Abe Fowler. The whole bunch spun as a unit and almost opened fire before Darby's shouts made them realize that he wasn't an Indian or an ambusher.

"What do you want?" the pigeon-toed man shouted.

"I want to talk."

"Then come on down. All of you."

They found a trail that led to the floor of the arroyo and when they joined the party below, Darby noticed three fresh graves.

"Poisoned?"

"By lead," Fowler said in a harsh voice. He looked all

around. "Where are your stinking camels? The last thing we need is for our stock to panic and run away."

"Tell us what happened to your men," Darby said.

"We got to drinking and there was some brag. I went to sleep about midnight, as did most of the others. Next thing we know, all hell is broke loose and bullets are flying thicker'n mosquitoes."

"Did the three shoot each other?"

"Well, I ain't rightly sure," Fowler admitted.

Darby frowned. "What does that mean?"

"It means our men died with some pretty big rifle slugs in 'em."

Darby waited for more. When Fowler didn't continue, Darby said, "And?"

"And none of the boys went for their rifles!"

Darby blinked, then glanced at his friends. Zack and Bear shuffled over to study the graves, their faces impassive, but Dolly said exactly what was on everyone's mind. "Are you saying that these men might have been ambushed?"

"Yeah, that's exactly what I'm sayin'."

"Any idea who did the killing?"

"Nope. There were five other outfits in this arroyo last night. Could have been any one of them or some other one that was camped close by."

"What are you going to do now?" Darby asked.

"That's what we was asking ourselves just now," Fowler said. "We were just about to take a vote."

"Don't let us stop you."

"We won't."

Darby and Dolly joined Zack and Bear. In less than a minute, a vote was taken and Fowler's outfit decided to return to Virginia City.

"You heard the vote," Fowler said, sounding extremely discouraged. "I voted to go on but the men have come to believe this whole deal is snake-bit. And once that notion gets in someone's mind real strong, they're whipped."

"I'm sorry," Darby said, "about the vote and about those dead men."

"They were good boys. Are you going on with those camels?"

"You bet we are," Dolly said. "The camels are just starting to warm up."

"Take a piece of honest advice," Fowler said earnestly, "turn those camels loose in this desert and come back with us before you die too. There'll be more killing. Mark my words."

"There has been already," Darby replied. He told Fowler and the others about the outfit that had been poisoned.

Fowler swallowed and appeared to be badly shaken. He shook his head hopelessly and said, "Someone is out to kill off the competition, that's for sure. That's all the more reason for you to return with us to the Comstock Lode instead of dying out here by yourselves."

But Darby thought differently. "Was young Alexander Poole around when this happened?"

"Nope. Musta been up in the forefront with the leaders."

Darby frowned. He stuck out his fist and shook Fowler's hand, saying, "Good luck."

"You're the one that'll need it if you don't turn those cussed camels loose and come along to Virginia City."

"We've got luck," Dolly said, forcing some spirit into her voice. "You see, Darby and I both saw a shooting star."

Fowler pulled off his Stetson and scratched a bald pate. "Huh?"

"Never mind," Darby said, taking Dolly's arm and heading away.

"But you didn't let me tell him about luck and shooting stars," Dolly protested.

"Why bother?" Darby said. "His luck just ran out."

Fourteen

DARBY AND THE REST plodded on for another four days
without seeing a living thing except for a bunch of wild burros
and mules that brayed at them from a distant rocky hilltop.

"There must be some water in this country," Darby said
that evening as they made another dry camp.

"Oh, there was," Zack said bitterly. "But you'll notice that
both water holes we came upon were sucked so dry there
weren't nothing left but baked mud. I told you we should've
run with the pack."

"No," Dolly said in Darby's defense. "If we had tried to do
that, we'd have been the ones poisoned or shot by now."

"She's right," Bear grumbled. "Besides, Zack, you said
yourself that we're making up time now that we don't have to
pull a wagon in this sandy country. How many places did we
see where they had to dig wagons out today?"

"Oh, three or four, I expect," Zack said.

"More like six or seven," Darby corrected, lighting a cigar
and passing a bottle of brandy and cigars around.

Dolly stared into the campfire, content to relax beside the
Derby Man while he and his rough companions sipped a little
brandy and smoked their cigars. This had become a nightly
ritual and it seemed to Dolly to be an important one. Darby
had confided, however, that both the brandy and the cigars
would run out about the time they reached Gold Peak.

"Hey, Emil!" Zack shouted out into the darkness toward
their sage-devouring camels. "Emil, why don't you come in
here and join the human race?"

"He prefers the company of his stinking camels," Bear said.

"Or his own company," Dolly added.

"Or the absence of the hounds," Darby said.

Zack scowled. "I never knew an Arab before. They are strange little buggers, ain't they?"

Darby prodded the campfire into risen life. "Emil is just different."

"Maybe he misses his own people in Arabia. Maybe," Dolly said heavily, "he wishes he'd never come to America. If he hadn't, he'd probably have his own camels, maybe a wife and children, too. I think that's why he acts sad and goes off by himself sometimes. He wants a wife and children."

Darby felt the focus of Dolly's gaze and squirmed. Looking across the campfire, he said to the mountain men, "How much farther to Gold Peak?"

"Forty miles or less."

"And judging from the tracks, how far ahead are the others?"

"My guess is less than half that," Zack answered. Bear nodded in silent agreement.

"Excuse me," Dolly said, coming to her feet and heading out to visit Emil.

Bear snorted. "I don't know why she bothers talking to an Arab."

Zack surprised everyone when he said, "Because she's got a good heart, Bear. A damned good heart."

The rebuke stung and Bear reacted in anger. "Well, you don't have to tell me that!"

"Simmer down, boys," Darby said.

The three of them smoked their cigars for almost an hour and when Dolly finally returned, she said, "Emil feels very bad, Darby. I was right about him—he misses his home country and wishes he had his own camels and a family."

The three men smoked on that without comment. Dolly finally said, "Boys, if we get this contract, perhaps we could send Emil back to Arabia with Mohammed and enough money to get a good start."

"Don't be ridiculous," Darby said. "You don't ship camels from America to Arabia. If anything, we'd give him enough money to go home and buy a few one-humped Arabian camels."

"To hell with that," Zack said around his cigar, "if we win the contract, we'll need Emil El Babba to handle those ornery two-humpers. Be purty stupid to send him home. That'd leave us up the creek without a paddle."

"He's right," Bear said.

"All you men think about is money!" Dolly exploded. She stomped off in a huff to roll up in her blankets and go to sleep.

Bear and Zack looked to Darby but he avoided their quizzical faces and studied the fire. "Fame and fortune," he said, more to himself than to them, "are mere illusion."

"Huh?" Zack asked.

Darby hurled the stump of his cigar into the flames. "Never mind," he said, climbing to his feet and going to bed.

THE FOLLOWING DAY they crossed some long stretches of deep sand which the camels handled with ease. In fact, they seemed to prefer the sand to the rocky country they'd been accustomed to negotiating in the eastern Sierras and the Comstock. Darby noted that the camel's great round footpads expanded under the beast's considerable weight. In passing, even the smaller camels left footprints bigger than Bear's open hand, and Mohammed's prints were larger than serving plates.

At midday, they stopped and rested for an hour and refilled their canteens from their water barrels. Darby noticed how flushed Dolly's face was becoming and advised her to keep it shaded from the blazing sun.

"It must be well over a hundred," Bear said, mopping his forehead with his wet shirt sleeve.

"I'd guess it's a hundred and ten in the shade, if there was any to be found," Darby said, studying the low, shimmering badlands flowing out into arid infinity. "This is the hardest country I've ever seen. Worse by far than the Apache country down in Arizona and New Mexico."

"No sign of Paiutes," Dolly said, ever promoting the bright side of even the bleakest situation. "I feel so sorry for those Indians having to live in this awful country."

"They could move," Bear said. "Go up to the mountains west of here where it's cooler. They must enjoy roasting in this hell's kitchen."

"Let's get the camels and get out of here," Darby said.

No one really wanted to move, but in summertime you did not remain stationary in the sun very long if you wanted to live. That afternoon, a hot, suffocating wind arose in the east and hurled tumbleweeds and sand with maniacal force until it was impossible to see or breathe. Emil turned Mohammed's back to it and ordered the camel to drop to the ground. Then the Arab helped the others do the same and they all crouched behind the beasts for cover as the sand scoured the desert for more than two hours.

When the sandstorm passed, Darby watched its great cloud obliterate the horizon as it swept off toward the distant Sierra Nevada Mountains. Emil climbed back on Mohammed and they continued on for the rest of the afternoon, minute particles of blown sand chafing raw every joint, wrinkle and orifice of their bodies.

Just before sundown, Emil spied a tall stand of creosote bush and reined Mohammed toward the evening's camel fodder. After dismounting, they realized that another party of freight wagons was returning from the south.

"Wonder which bunch this is?" Zack asked.

"We'll soon find out," Darby said. "They've spotted us and they ought to be here shortly after sundown."

Darby and the mountain men gathered deadfall from the desert floor and dragged it into a pile. "Put a match to it," Darby ordered. "Let's give them a beacon."

When the sun began to slip into the curve of the earth, the temperature did drop, but not appreciably. It hovered at well

over one hundred degrees and the desert baked like sheep-
herder's bread in a Dutch oven.

It was an hour after dark when about twenty wagons came
slogging through the sand and halted about a quarter mile
from the camp.

"Are you the outfit with the camels?" a voice called out of
the starlight.

"That's right."

"Well, Mr. Buckingham, we don't want our stock to stampede, so we'll make a camp and come on over afoot."

"Suit yourselves," Darby shouted.

An hour later, a dozen sweaty, beaten men came straggling
into camp. "My name is Theodore Lawler," the one in
charge said. "Can you spare a little water?"

"Help yourself," Darby said, pointing toward the most re-
cently opened water barrel.

Lawler and his companions threw themselves at the water
barrel. Ignoring the dipper, they used cupped hands to drink
their fill and because of their raging thirst, they spilled about
as much as they consumed. Darby glanced sideways and could
see that Dolly was shocked by the suffering written into these
men's haggard faces.

When they were finished, Darby said, "You can take the
rest of that barrel back with you."

Lawler closed his eyes and took a deep breath. He looked
to be in pretty rough shape.

"You all right?" Darby asked.

"No," Lawler said, opening his eyes. "None of us are all
right, but we're still alive. You see, yesterday we buried four
good men."

"Were they poisoned?" Darby asked quietly.

Lawler's expression turned murderous. "Hell no! They
were goaded into a fight by Bert Jasper and his gunnies. It
wasn't much of a contest. Our boys aren't professional gunfighters. It was a slaughter."

"I see." Darby sighed. "Tell me, how many freight companies are still in the running?"

"Three or four. I dunno. They've banded together to protect themselves against Jasper and his men."

"What about Alexander Poole?" Darby asked. "He's supposed to be the . . ."

Lawler snorted with derision. "He's scared stiff of Bert Jasper! Why, you can hear his knees knocking for a hundred miles."

"Is he with Jasper?"

"No. He's with them other freighters I was telling you banded together. But they're fools. Jasper and his men are killers and they'll cut them down to size."

Zack stepped up close. "How far ahead are they all?"

"Not far. The road is so bad we were spending more time trying to keep from burying our wagons to the axles than we were making tracks to Gold Peak. That goddamn Arthur Poole fed us a line when he said that the road was good and solid except for the last six or seven miles! I wouldn't take this supply run on contract with the Comstock Mining Company for *ten* thousand dollars a month!"

"We wouldn't either," Zack said, "without a string of camels."

Lawler gazed into the darkness, finding the dark silhouettes of the Comstock camels contentedly munching sage in the starlight. He shook his head in utter amazement and when he spoke, there was a touch of irony in his voice.

"Mr. Buckingham, maybe this is the one stretch of hell long and dry enough to warrant the existence of camels. And, to be honest, I would far rather you camel lovers win that contract than Bert Jasper and his gang of murderers."

"You got any food for yourselves or your livestock?" Dolly asked.

"Not much," Lawler admitted, dropping his eyes.

Darby knew that he could not let these men or their livestock die. "We'll leave you a few bales of hay and another barrel of water. I hope it's enough to get you out of this country alive."

"You're all right, Buckingham," Lawler said, raising his

chin to meet Darby's eyes and sticking out his hand. "I'm sorry for all the mean-spirited things we've said about you and the camels."

"I ain't sorry about hatin' camels," one of Lawler's men blurted. "I hate 'em now, I'll hate 'em until I die. But I hate Bert Jasper and his gunnies even more."

Darby, Bear and Zack shook hands all around and then they gave Lawler's outfit some food and water and watched them trudge back to their camp.

"Sounds like the competition is being whittled down for us right sudden like, don't it?" Bear said to the Derby Man.

"I'm afraid so, but it doesn't surprise me."

"You should've killed Big Bert instead of just whupped him to a nubbin back in Virginia City."

Darby said nothing. Instead he watched the dark silhouettes of the men struggle back across the cooking desert. Bear was probably right, but it was a terrible thing to beat a man to death with your fists. In all his years of bare knuckles fighting, Darby had never killed a man that way, but he'd seen it happen once and it had left an indelible mark on his soul.

Seeing the Derby Man's wintery expression, Dolly came to his aid. She hugged his shrinking waistline and noted the deep weariness in his posture and voice. Even his handsome face had lost its rosy roundness because of this heat and unrelenting hardship.

"Come on," she said. "You look tired and in need of sleep."

But Darby shook his head. "Not yet. We haven't had our cigars and brandy yet."

"Save them for tomorrow night," Dolly said, pulling him off toward his blanket. "Tonight we can hold hands and watch for shooting stars."

"Are you saying we need a little more good luck?"

Dolly dipped her chin. "Yes," she said, "I think we could use all that we can get in the days to come, don't you?"

"Most certainly," Darby said, linking his arm through hers and heading for his blankets.

Fifteen

HIGH ATOP HIS CAMEL, Darby sweated and squinted, rocked and rolled as heat waves distorted the ravaged face of the heat-stricken desert. Darby could not imagine how anything lived out in this devil's playground, yet every morning at daybreak, he found fresh evidence of the nocturnal wanderings of coyotes, turtles, foxes, squirrels and rabbits. Before the sun broke from the bowl of the earth, scorpions scuttled across the sands for shade and rattlesnakes slithered into the lifesaving coolness of their deep underground burrows. During the morning, before the heat became so oppressive, birds flitted through the sky and tittered in the branches while, high overhead, hawks and vultures soared effortlessly. Insects were annoyingly plentiful and the damned things all either bit or stung with authority.

To Darby's way of thinking, the only redeeming feature of a desert was its sunrises and sunsets. At daybreak, rainbow colors swam brilliantly across the eastern horizon. For a few glorious moments, clouds emblazoned the sky in a moment of unearthly splendor. Desert sunsets were no less breathtaking, each a unique and magnificent canvas. But during the rest of summer's waking hours, a desert was God's best reminder and preview of hell.

Darby's eyes burned despite the wide-brimmed canvas hat he had opted for instead of his pathetic derby. The sun's reflection off the sand was so intense that it fried one's skin and made one weak and giddy. How much farther to Gold Peak? Would they survive this blistering purgatory?

At mid-afternoon, when the heat was so intense that it burned to breathe, Emil suddenly drew Mohammed to a halt. Darby's camel stopped so abruptly that he nearly toppled over its neck.

"What the deuce is it?" Bear shouted from behind.

Emil did not answer but instead raised his hand and pointed. Through the undulating heat waves, Darby saw a vision of many men, beasts and wagons. "That's our competition," he said to himself. "We've finally overtaken them—and Jasper."

The camels began to squawk and move faster, though Darby could not imagine why. He yanked the shotgun from his saddle and made the mistake of touching its trigger and searing his index finger. Darby covered it with a piece of canvas and hoped that he would not require the weapon before it cooled.

Darby squinted hard to see the road's end, where about fifty high-sided wagons and a few canvas shades rigged up on poles waited in the blistering sun. Knots of men rested in the shade. Tied to picket lines were dozens of horses, mules and the pack string of burros that Darby had seen leaving Virginia City.

There must have been a slight breeze because the livestock up ahead suddenly twisted, scenting the approaching camels. They were so debilitated by the heat they hadn't the strength to panic. There was, however, a great deal of braying and neighing and men who had been reposing in the shade jumped up to keep their livestock from breaking loose.

Darby studied the flushed, sullen faces of these men. Some of them he recognized as members of Bert Jasper's crew; the others were from the remaining competing outfits.

"I better talk with them," Darby said, cueing his camel to drop to its knees in the hot sand as he uncovered his shotgun.

"We'll go with you," Bear offered.

Darby waited until he was joined by the two mountain men. Dolly remained atop her camel. "Be careful," she warned.

"Goes without saying," Darby replied, moving forward. "Anyone in charge here?"

A redheaded man in his early forties pushed out from the group and he was joined by a lean, hawk-faced man with a tie-down gun.

Zack leaned toward Darby and hissed, "Red Baker is a back-shooter and ambusher. Don't worry about him."

"What about the other man?"

"Frank Ketchem is snake-quick and bold as brass. He'll go for leather if he's pushed and his outfit will stand behind him."

Darby focused on Frank Ketchem, making sure that his shotgun was pointed in the lean man's direction. "It looks like your wagons have gone as far as they'll go. I expect you sent mules on to Gold Peak?"

Ketchem spat a thin stream of tobacco into the hot sand. "You can expect any damn thing you want, Mr. Buckingham."

"We're going on to Gold Peak," Darby said after a long pause. "So if you've plans to try and stop us or our camels, I think you might as well act now."

"What do you say, Red?" Frank asked out of the side of his mouth. "Why don't we take 'em right now?"

"With him holding a double-barreled shotgun?" Red shook his head back and forth. "No thanks."

"He's right," Darby said. "There's no sense in anyone getting killed. All we want is a fair chance to win this race."

Ketchem spat again and studied the shotgun, then the Hawken rifles in the capable hands of the mountain men. Finally, he said, "You pass on by, Mr. Derby Man. We'll be seeing you again."

"Is that a threat?" Zack asked quietly.

Ketchem's eyes narrowed and he stared hard at Zack. "Old man, it's anything you want it to be."

"In that case," Zack said, dropping his big buffalo rifle in line with Ketchem's chest, "I take it as a threat. Say your prayers, pilgrim."

Ketchem's only reaction was that his eyes widened a little.

But he didn't show any other sign of fear. "Old man, if you drill me, you and your outfit will be dead inside ten seconds."

"Let him be," Bear said.

"Yes," Darby urged. "Just let it go, Zack."

The old mountain man watched as the men beside the wagons picked up their own rifles. Zack didn't move a muscle and, in the moments that followed, the tension was so great that sweat poured out of Darby until Zack finally yielded.

Before he left to return to his camel, he said to Ketchem, "We've come across a lot of good men that have already been poisoned or shot. Before you throw in with Bert Jasper and his crew, I'd think about that."

"I've thought about it," Ketchem said. "And since Jasper hates your guts, maybe we'll just give him first chance at you and those camels. Either you kill him or he kills you—either way, we come out ahead."

Darby looked to Red. "What about you?"

"You ain't seen or heard the last of me."

"That's what I thought you'd say, back-shooter," Zack hissed.

Red's cheeks flamed but he didn't act upon the insult.

"Let's go on to Gold Peak," Darby said, backing toward his camel.

When they circumvented the men and wagons, a few of the teamsters glared and shook their fists in anger. Darby ignored them. Since he had not seen Jasper, that meant he, Alexander Poole and others had taken mules and gone on to Gold Peak to deliver supplies and haul back the required ore to these wagons.

Two hours later, Emil raised his hand and pointed toward a nondescript mountain. Gold Peak was neither large nor tall. It had no distinguishing features nor even an interesting profile. Rather, Gold Peak jutted like ridged knuckles from the desert floor. Darby could not imagine how Pokey Smith had chosen it over hundreds of other mountain ranges or stubby peaks washboarding this vast desert floor.

As for the mining camp itself, Darby observed a few tents

and a large canvas stretched out before the entrance to the mine shaft. There was a line of about fifty mules starting under the canvas shade. As Darby watched, men emerged from the mine entrance with heavy sacks of ore, which they packed onto the lead mules. As soon as a mule was loaded, it was led away and tied in the sun while another mule was pulled forward to await its heavy cargo of ore.

"It'll take them quite a while and a lot of trips back and forth to the wagons to load five tons per outfit," Darby said.

"I ain't too excited about loading five tons for ourselves," Bear grumbled.

"It won't take but three or four hours," Darby assured them. "When those mules are loaded and gone, we'll have Emil bring the camels right up to the mine entrance, unpack the supplies we've promised to deliver, then load up the ore and be on our way."

"What about the hay and the barrels of water?" Zack asked.

Darby had been fretting over that and there was only one unpleasant conclusion to be reached. "We're going to have to leave some behind in order to take back our five tons of ore. The important thing is that we get loaded and out headed back to the Comstock Lode quickly. We either get a big lead now, or we'll lose the race on the home stretch."

"We'll have trouble here," Bear said. "That tall man standing in the shade has got to be Jasper and he sure ain't going to welcome us with a glass of cool water."

"We'll handle Jasper and these men the same way we handled Ketchem and Red," Darby said, producing his shotgun a second time from under its protective canvas.

Jasper and the men at Gold Peak spotted them when their mules caught the disagreeable scent of the camels. Darby witnessed a flurry of excitement, then the loading of the mules was resumed as Jasper and his crew grabbed their rifles and waited in the shade.

Darby wondered if Alexander Poole was among the men up ahead. If so, he had knuckled under to Jasper's authority and would be no help. On the other hand, perhaps he had already been murdered, his body disposed of somewhere on the trail. Darby broke the shotgun and checked the double loads. Satisfied, he snapped the weapon closed in a hard show of determination.

"Look at Emil," Bear said to no one in particular, "he's fixin' to fight too!"

It was true. The Arabian blunderbuss was cradled across Emil's left forearm while he guided Mohammed onward.

Bert Jasper and his gunmen stepped out of the shade and came forward, hatbrims pulled low over their eyes. From the looks of them, it seemed clear that they were determined not to let the camels within fifty yards of the mules.

"We're going to be sitting ducks up this high," Bear warned.

Darby knew that Bear was right. He sawed on his camel's jaw rope, brought it to a halt and then tapped its leg. The beast hissed and folded down in front, big knee pads striking the burning sand. When its back end followed, Darby jumped and landed rather awkwardly but managed to stay erect. He cocked both hammers of his shotgun and started forward. Darby knew he was a lousy shot but if he could get close enough, his scatter gun would more than compensate for his lack of marksmanship.

Bear, Zack and Emil rushed to his side and, even though they were outnumbered three to one, they must have looked formidable because Jasper and his gunfighters didn't appear too happy with the way things were unfolding.

"Far enough," Jasper bellowed.

But the Derby Man kept walking. His double-barreled equalizer required close range.

Jasper gulped, looked at his companions and then back at Darby. "What the hell . . ."

Darby threw his shotgun to his shoulder. He was in range now, though it was probably still too far for the shot to be lethal.

"Unbuckle your guns," Darby yelled, "all of you!"

"Go to hell!" a man shouted, drawing his pistol.

It was only halfway out when Bear's huge buffalo rifle roared. The misguided gunfighter caught a load of lead in the chest. His body jumped ten feet back as if he'd been jerked backward by an invisible wire.

Bear dropped to one knee and began to reload with lightning speed. Darby kept marching forward. "Unbuckle and drop those guns, I say!"

"All right! All right!" Jasper shouted when Zack threw his buffalo rifle to his shoulder and took aim.

"You were here first," Darby said. "Finish loading your mules and then leave."

"There's another string coming in at dusk," Jasper cried in protest.

"They'll have to wait until we get our camels loaded," Zack said.

"Damn you!" Jasper raged. "You picked the time when half of my men are still out at the wagons. But later . . ."

Zack's left eye squeezed shut as he sighted on Jasper's broad chest.

"No!" the giant cried, jumping back into the mine entrance.

"Let him be," Darby said, turning to get Dolly.

"What are we going to do now?" Bear called to Darby.

"Rest under that canvas shade until those mules are loaded before we get to work," Darby replied. "What else did you expect?"

Bear shrugged, glanced at Zack, and the two of them strolled across the white-hot sand to take their places under the canvas. The mules snorted nervously because the mountain men smelled of camel. But the smell had become a natural part of Zack and Bear, so much so that they weren't even aware of it anymore.

When Darby helped Dolly down from her camel, she was faint from the heat so he picked her up in his arms and carried her to rest under the canvas. Someone brought her a canteen.

Its water was wonderfully cool, for it had been stored in oak barrels inside the mine tunnel.

"Thanks," Darby said.

He squatted on his heels. "You must be the Derby Man."

"That's right."

"Mr. Poole told me about you. Said you were a good man but you'd never live to reach our camp."

"Where is he?"

"Inside the tunnel." The man extended his hand. "My name is Carl Hanson. I'm the foreman of this operation."

Darby shook the foreman's hand but his mind was distracted. "Tell me about young Alexander."

"He's in bad shape. Real bad. Must have drank some poisoned water. He's mostly out of his mind."

Darby ground his teeth in anger. "How long has he been like that?"

"Since Jasper and his men brought him here."

Darby waited until Dolly had her fill of the canteen and then he motioned Zack and Bear to come to watch over her.

"I'm going inside to see Alexander," he said. "Don't drop your guard for a minute."

"Don't worry," Bear said, watching as the mules were loaded. "This is hard, hard company."

Darby tapped Hanson on the sleeve. "Take me to Alexander right now!"

"All right, but he's still delirious. Ain't a thing anyone can do for him now except the Almighty."

Darby's stomach knotted with anxiety. With his shotgun balanced lightly in his hands and Dolly pressing close behind, he followed Hanson into the maw of the mine.

Sixteen

THE MINE TUNNEL ran at a slight upward incline for about two hundred feet into Gold Peak where it terminated in a barn-sized cavern. Kerosene lamps illuminated the cavern, revealing bright veins of quartz and sprinklings of silver and gold. At the base of the working face of the cavern lay a mountainous pile of loose rock. This ore was being loaded into wheelbarrows and hauled out to the waiting mules. It was hard, brutal work but at least the temperature was bearable.

Miner's supplies were piled high along the west wall of the cavern and Alexander Poole lay on a straw mattress pressed up against the opposite wall. In the fluttering, oily light of the lamps, Darby studied the young man's drawn face.

"Alexander," Darby whispered. "Alexander!"

The young man moaned softly and his lips trembled, but he said nothing and his skin was feverish to the touch.

"How is he?" Dolly asked, kneeling by their side.

"Bad," Darby said. "I'm not sure if he's taken the same poison as those other men that died on the trail, but I wouldn't be surprised."

"Oh," Dolly whispered, "let's pray that isn't the case or he's doomed!"

Hanson sighed. "He's been like this since yesterday. His breathing is shallow, his pulse racing, his fever will not break."

"Have you given him any medicine?"

Hanson shrugged. "We've tried to get a little sulfa powder in solution down his throat, but I don't think we were successful. We have no quinine nor much in the way of medicines. Just some bandages and splints. I did send an old Paiute who scavenges wood for our cooking fires off to see if his people will give us any Indian medicines."

Darby wasn't greatly heartened by this news. It wasn't that he thought Indian medicines were worthless, for he knew better. It was just that Darby seriously doubted the unfriendly Paiutes were interested in helping a deathly ill white man.

"I don't know what else to do," Hanson said, with a worried and bewildered expression on his lean face. "And I can't begin to understand why Mr. Poole would have risked his life to come down here in the first place."

"It's a long story," Darby said, turning so that his back was toward the rock wall and his shotgun was pointed toward Jasper's wheelbarrow brigade. "Suffice to say, young Alexander felt he had something to prove."

Hanson's eyebrows arched in question but Darby chose to say no more. There was, in his opinion, a very good possibility that Alexander was going to die and it served no honorable purpose to go into the reasons why his father had felt it so important that his pampered son make this hard and dangerous trip to Gold Peak.

Darby looked up at the mine foreman. "How long will it take Jasper's men to load their mules?"

"At the rate they are working, about four more hours. But like Jasper said, by then there will be another string to take their place."

"They'll have to wait in line until we're finished," Darby said.

Dolly plucked at his sleeve. "But what about this young man? He's too sick to move and we can't just leave him behind."

"We might have to," Darby said. "You know our water situation. Even a few days' delay would place an additional hardship on the camels before we can return to the Walker River. And don't forget, we are in a race."

"The contract isn't worth this man's life. We must put Alexander's health and welfare before that of our camels."

"If Mr. Poole can survive this," Hanson said in a placating tone of voice, "he can remain here until the weather cools and return to the Comstock with a supply wagon."

Darby looked at Dolly. "Be reasonable, my dear. We can't take Alexander out in this heat if he's feverish. It would finish him for certain."

Dolly managed to dip her chin in reluctant agreement. "I just feel so . . . so helpless."

"We all do," Hanson said. "Until Bert Jasper arrived with poor Mr. Poole strapped to the back of a mule and half out of his mind with fever, we thought we were suffering from this terrible heat. Seeing Mr. Poole made me and my crew realize that things can always get a lot worse."

"Amen," Darby said. He turned away from the feverish young mine owner and studied the walls of the cavern. "Is it a strike?"

Hanson managed a thin smile. "It's as promising as anything I've seen on the Comstock Lode. Indications are that the ore contains more silver than gold but it is still plenty rich."

"The assay results are pretty good?"

"I can't reveal our exact figures," Hanson said, "but they are very promising. On the Comstock, the big mines like the Savage and Crown Point yielded about 54 percent gold and 46 percent silver but they're the exception. Most Comstock mines produce twice the value of silver to gold."

"I had no idea that the silver was worth more than the gold."

"Oh, it isn't!" Hanson said. "It's just that it's more plentiful. If silver prices stay at $1.29 an ounce, we can't miss. As for the gold, well, if it's an even moderately rich strike, it will yield $3,500 a ton."

Hanson winked almost conspiratorially. "Between you and me, I think this ore also has substantial percentages of zinc, lead, copper and antimony—all valuable minerals that we can recapture during the refining process."

Darby wasn't comfortable with figures, but these made him sit up and blink. "Why, at $3,500 a ton, with each of us bringing back five tons to your stamping mills at Silver City, this so-called 'race' is going to prove extremely profitable to the Comstock Mining Company."

"I just heard about it," Hanson admitted. "And yes, it will earn a substantial profit. The senior Mr. Poole would not have it any other way. He didn't get rich by losing money, you know."

"Of course not."

"And," Hanson added, "remember that mining costs are very, very high. Especially here at Gold Peak, where we're forced to pay our miners triple wages in order to lure them off the Comstock Lode. Even then they want to return after just a few short weeks. They can't, of course. If they tried it on their own, they'd die."

Darby understood completely. No amount of money could have induced him into this hellish desert. What *had* brought him to Gold Peak was the chance to finally get Zack and Bear established in a profitable enterprise. Besides, Darby could not possibly have allowed Miss Beavers to risk so much hardship and danger without his constant protection. And he actually had been penning a few notes about this race and realizing that, with a few literary liberties, it might—just might—prove interesting enough to use for the basis of his next dime novel.

Darby heard a loud shout outside. Fearing that Zack and Bear might have been overpowered by Jasper's men, he rushed back down the tunnel with the shotgun clenched in his fist to discover that the commotion was due to the appearance of seven Paiute Indians.

Hanson was right on Darby's heels. When he saw the Indians with their crude bows and arrows were about to be fired upon by Jasper's gunmen, he yelled, "Don't shoot them! They're friendlies!"

Everyone stared as the mining foreman rushed into the line of fire waving his arms and yelling at the top of his voice. When Hanson reached out to the Indians, he began to communicate using more hand gestures than words. A moment later, he led two of the Paiutes back to the mine.

"This is Oh-tah and Waa-so-ah," he announced to everyone. "Oh-tah gathers wood for the Comstock Mining Company and Waa-so-ah is his tribal medicine man. They have come to help Mr. Poole."

"Oh yeah?" Jasper challenged. "Well, I say they're more likely to poison him!"

"You'd know all about that sort of thing, wouldn't you?" Bear growled.

The giant swung around and the two powerful men glared at each other. Bear's fists knotted and he started toward the giant but Darby jumped between them.

"Out of my way," Bear commanded.

"Back off!" Darby said angrily. "We need you and Zack to stand guard, not to get into a brawl or a gunfight."

When the two big men had simmered down, Darby escorted the Paiutes into the tunnel and trailed along behind them ready to use his shotgun at the slightest hint of trouble. Upon reaching Alexander's side, the Paiute medicine man studied the patient for a full minute before he dropped to one knee. Waa-so-ah touched Alexander's cheek, then rolled back his eyelid to study his pupils. He placed his ear to Alexander's chest and gently palpated his stomach.

He spoke rapidly to Oh-tah and the Indian turned and raced up the tunnel.

"What did he say?" Darby asked, watching the wood gatherer disappear.

Hanson shook his head. "They're speaking too fast. I only know a few words of their language. Just enough to direct Oh-tah in his work."

"I see."

As Darby watched, the Paiute medicine man unslung a leather pouch containing small bunches of herbs. He spread them out on the cave's floor as if they were a collection of rare and precious gems. Darby recognized sage blossoms and one or two other plants' flowers and leaves, but he was unfamiliar with most. The medicine man began to select different herbs, sometimes picking one up, then after long consideration reluctantly setting it back down.

When he had chosen a small, select assortment, Waa-so-ah closed his eyes, threw his long braided hair back, then began to chant. He rocked back and forth on his knees, eyes focused on the glittering overhead dome of rich minerals. His fingers, short, bony, but quick and nimble, began to stir and pluck the herbs from the stone floor. Clapping his hands together and with the laugh of a playful child, Waa-so-ah began to rub his palms together until the herbs sifted back to the floor as powder. At just that moment, Oh-tah returned with a skin of very dark liquid.

Waa-so-ah made a potion of his herbs, then jumped up and began to chant and shake the mixture overhead as he danced.

"Why doesn't he just give it to him?" Dolly asked impatiently.

Hanson overheard her and answered, "These Indian cures rely as much on ritual as the actual medicine itself. This dancing and chanting are the ritualistic parts. Waa-so-ah is beseeching the Indian spirits to make the medicine strong enough to drive out the sickness and fever."

"Oh," Dolly said, as she joined Darby in watching the medicine man dance around and around in the smoky light of the kerosene lamps.

The chanting was an unintelligible monotone but Darby was mesmerized by Waa-so-ah's grace, precision and intensity. Without conscious thought, the Derby Man gathered paper and pencil from his shirt pocket and began to scribble notes. He used action verbs and rich, colorful adjectives which, like planted seeds, would lie fallow until called upon to sprout into visual images from the depths of his fertile mind.

The medicine man and the wood gatherer were probably only in their thirties, yet both were as wrinkled as ancient

Egyptian mummies. They wore the scantiest of breechcloths made of rabbit skins and Waa-so-ah was decorated with feathers and a necklace of coyote claws. The ritualistic dance and chanting continued long enough for Darby to smoke a cigar and scribble several pages of notes for the dime novel he now felt compelled to write about the Comstock camels. When the dance stopped, it was so abrupt that Darby was startled from his reverie. Waa-so-ah barked something to his companion and Oh-tah knelt at Alexander's side. He slipped one thin brown hand under Alexander's neck, forcing his mouth open with the other.

Waa-so-ah poured his herbal medicine down Alexander's throat without spilling a drop. When Alexander choked and threatened to spit the liquid up, the medicine man used the heel of his hand to drive Alexander's lower jaw into his upper one so tightly that the white man had no choice but to swallow the medicine.

It was done. Waa-so-ah beamed and did a strange and interesting thing. He bowed to Dolly and Darby before he turned to the mining foreman. It took quite some time for Hanson to understand what the Paiute medicine man wanted and even then he was not sure he understood correctly.

"What is he saying, Mr. Hanson?"

"I think he says he and his friends want to ride the camels."

"No!"

Waa-so-ah stepped back, looking very offended by the sharp tone of Darby's voice. He spoke rapidly to the wood gatherer, who spoke in turn to the mine foreman, who then spoke again to Darby.

"No question about it," Hanson said. "Waa-so-ah and his people wish to ride the camels and then take one in repayment for his services."

"Impossible!" Dolly cried. "In the first place, we have no idea if this Indian medicine did a thing for poor Mr. Poole's fever. And in the second place, even if it did, Emil El Babba would never give up a camel."

"In that case," Hanson said grimly, "we'll have a full-scale Paiute uprising right outside the mine."

"We can handle them," Darby said.

"Quite probably you can," Hanson said, looking very upset. "I'm sure that if you and Mr. Jasper could settle your differences long enough to combine forces, you could kill a great number of Paiutes. But after you are gone, they would kill us to the last man. Is that what you want?"

"Of course not."

"Then you must grant the Paiute medicine man his request."

Darby shook his head. "Not until we see if the medicine did any good. That's only reasonable. Waa-so-ah will understand that. Every culture withholds payment until there is some kind of satisfaction rendered."

Hanson shook his head. "I . . ."

"Tell him," Darby insisted, "that we will only let him ride a camel if Alexander's fever breaks because of his medicine."

Hanson was very displeased but Darby did not care. It took nearly a quarter of an hour to make the medicine man understand and then Waa-so-ah was extremely upset. He and the wood gatherer marched outside and joined the other Paiutes, who waited just beyond rifle range.

Darby listened to their angry words, then marched back into the tunnel saying to Jasper, "Finish loading these damn mules and get them out of here! We're wasting time."

Darby knelt beside Alexander. He touched the young man's face. His flesh was still hot.

Dolly came to sit beside him. "Do you think the Paiute medicine did any good?"

"I have no idea," Darby said, closing his eyes and drinking in the coolness of the mountain's hard core. "But any cure takes at least a few hours. Let's give it some time."

He awoke to feel Dolly shaking his shoulder and yelling, "The fever is gone! It's broken, Darby! Look!"

Darby was so drugged by exhaustion that it took him several minutes to regain his senses. When he did, he was amazed to see that the young mining executive had not only regained his color, but was actually staring at him with a weak smile.

"Well, well," Alexander said, "if it isn't the Derby Man himself."

"Good heavens, Alexander! We thought you were lost!"

"I feel very, very tired," Alexander said. "And weak. What happened?"

"That's what we'd like to know. Were you poisoned?"

Alexander blinked. He looked around wildly, fear springing to his eyes. "Is Jasper . . ."

"He's outside," Darby said. "And he's not a bit happy about this. He'll be even less happy when he discovers you are alive."

Alexander grabbed Darby's sleeve. "I think he's been poisoning everyone!"

"Think? Don't you know?"

Alexander shook his head. "I don't know," he whispered. "I guess I should, but I've never seen him actually do it."

"What about ambushing members of the other outfits?" Dolly asked.

"There's been ambushing?"

Darby swore under his breath. If Alexander had known, they might quickly get the drop on the giant and his gunmen, then tie them up and return the bunch of cutthroats to Virginia City under their constant guard. In a Nevada courtroom, they'd be found guilty of multiple murders and hanged. With luck, they could do all this without firing a single shot or shedding one ounce of blood.

At just that moment, Oh-tah appeared in the cavern. When he saw Alexander was awake and talking, he quickly returned with a beaming Hanson. Pointing and gesturing, the Paiute wood gatherer left no doubt in Darby's mind what he wanted.

Hanson confirmed this. "He says that Mr. Poole will live now and he wants us to be honorable and let his tribesman ride and then choose a camel."

Dolly shook her head. "Emil will . . ."

"Will have to accept the fact that he's only going to be in charge of eleven camels instead of a dozen," Darby said. "One camel is fair repayment and besides, to refuse would be to place Mr. Hanson and his crew in mortal danger from the Paiutes."

"He's right, Miss Beavers," Hanson seconded. "To refuse Waa-so-ah would be our death sentence."

Dolly sagged with acceptance. "All right, but I'd better be the one to break this news to Emil."

"All right," Darby said. "Tell him the camel is a gift in exchange for Mr. Poole's life. If he can understand that, perhaps he will accept this gracefully."

"I doubt it," Dolly said, heading out of the tunnel.

ONE BY ONE, Emil El Babba helped the Paiutes onto Mohammed's back while the other camels were being loaded with ore. It was well past midnight when the last of the Paiutes had had their short ride. Several of them, like Bear and Zack, had gotten sick. But unlike Bear and Zack, they'd giggled and made sport of their rioting stomachs.

"The camels are all packed except Mohammed," Bear announced. He was sweating and so weary from helping to carry and pack the five tons of ore they were to return to Silver City that he actually swayed on his feet.

Besides Mohammed, they had not loaded ore on two other, smaller camels. That meant, after the Paiutes took one camel, there would be two left to carry enough water and food to allow them to escape the desert.

Emil El Babba was a devastated man. He had argued vehemently against allowing the Paiutes to ride a camel, and then, when he learned he would have to give one up, he was reduced to angry tears.

"I just hope like crazy that they don't want Mohammed," Dolly whispered. "I wish Emil would have let the Indians ride some other camel."

"He wanted to," Darby confessed, "but I wouldn't allow it."

"Why?"

"Because I loathe Mohammed. I hope they soon roast him alive!"

Dolly's eyes dilated with anger and she looked ready to kill. Things didn't get any better a few moments later when the Paiutes indicated in no uncertain terms that it was indeed Mohammed that they wanted.

"Now look what you've done!" Dolly stormed as Emil drew his sword and prepared to fight to the death.

"Oh blast!" Darby swore as the Paiutes nocked their bow-strings with arrows.

Seventeen

DARBY WAS CAUGHT in a terrible fix. He knew that what happened in the next few moments would determine all of their fates. If Emil El Babba killed a Paiute, it would cause the others to attack and the result would be a bloodbath. No doubt he and Jasper's men could annihilate the Indians with their primitive bows and arrows. However, more would come and it would spell the end of mining in this part of Nevada as word of the slaughter spread among the fierce Paiutes faster than sand in a desert whirlwind.

"Emil!" Darby shouted, hurrying forward. "You have to give Mohammed to them!"

"No, boss! Emil die first!"

"If that happens, who will take care of the rest of your beautiful camels?"

"Zack and Bear."

"I don't think so," Darby said, advancing on the Arab, who now held his sword at the ready.

"Stand back, boss!" Emil warned.

Darby stopped about ten feet in front of the man. "Listen," he pleaded, "you're going to get us all killed over that big, stupid camel! You'll still have eleven others to take care of, so be reasonable."

"Mohammed my favorite camel!"

"Then you'd give up one of the others?"

Emil struggled. Tears filled his eyes and Darby's heart really went out to the little guy when he finally nodded in reluctant agreement.

Darby said to the mine foreman, "Explain to the Paiutes that they must take a different camel."

Hanson sighed. "You don't understand these people, Mr. Buckingham; once they . . ."

"Try and change their minds, Mr. Hanson," Darby commanded. "Our lives are in grave jeopardy."

Hanson went over to Waa-so-ah and tried hard to persuade the Paiute medicine man to choose another camel. But the Indian had eyes only for the biggest, strongest camel. Waa-so-ah kept stubbornly shaking his head and then pointing into the mouth of the cave. It was clear that he thought his price for saving Alexander Poole's life was only fair.

"He's not going to budge," Dolly said at last. "Emil, please! Mohammed is only a camel!"

Emil's eyes flashed with defiance. "Mohammed is finest camel in America!"

"That may well be," Darby said in his most reasonable tone of voice as he stepped in closer to the Arab, "but a camel's life is not worth that of a human being. I'm sure you would agree."

"No agree!"

Darby watched as the Arab tensed to strike. It was clear that Emil El Babba had lost his senses. He'd made a stand and was too proud to back down.

"All right," Darby said under his breath. "You can keep Mohammed."

"I can, boss?"

"Sure. We'll just kill all these Indians."

"Kill them?" Emil's sword dropped a few inches. "Very bad, boss!"

Darby shrugged. "No other choice."

Emil frowned and weighed this decision very carefully. Darby held his breath until Emil said, "You are right, boss. We kill all Indians."

"Oh blast," Darby muttered, swinging the butt of his shotgun. It was a move he'd used before with great effectiveness and which required powering the butt-stock with his right hand and then releasing and throwing it outward at the last instant.

The butt of the shotgun caught Emil under the jaw with such force that, when he collapsed, Darby thought he might have snapped the Arab's neck.

"Emil!" Dolly cried, running forward. She dropped to the Arab's side, then checked to see if he had a pulse and was breathing.

"Is he alive?" Darby asked.

"Yes, but no thanks to you!"

"I saw no other choice," Darby replied. He walked over to Mohammed. The great beast squawked and spat at him but missed. Grabbing Mohammed's jaw rope, Darby forced the animal to its knees.

"Waa-so-ah?"

Upon hearing his name, the medicine man puffed up. He jangled his coyote claws and raised his chin, to the admiration of his fellow tribesmen. Then, with great dignity, Waa-so-ah strutted forward and climbed aboard Mohammed, who tried to bite him and would have if Darby hadn't yanked on his rope. Squawking and hissing, Mohammed came to his feet and Darby motioned Oh-tah forward to take the rope.

"Tell them we wish them good luck," Darby said to Hanson. "And good eating."

"Huh?"

"Darby!" Dolly cried with outrage.

Darby sighed. "Just tell these Indians to get out of here before Emil El Babba regains his senses."

"Sure," Hanson said nervously.

With Oh-tah leading Mohammed and Waa-so-ah rocking high up on the camel's back, the Paiutes quickly made their departure. The other camels tried to follow their leader, but Sid and Slick seemed to understand the way of things and worked the eleven camels like sheep dogs. They snarled and snapped and drove the unhappy camels to distraction, causing them to quickly forget about Mohammed.

Darby tied the unconscious Arab hand and foot, then threw

him over one of the camels. Emil did not weigh much, but
what there was of him was muscle and backbone.

Jasper and his crew had already left with the mules and now
more were coming to be loaded when Darby went back inside
the mine.

"I'm coming with you," Alexander said, pushing himself
unsteadily to his feet.

"I don't think that would be a very good idea."

"I don't care what you think, Mr. Buckingham," Alexander
snapped. "I'm not staying here a minute longer than necessary."

"You aren't strong enough to travel in the heat."

"Oh yes I am!" He took a faltering step toward Darby,
then had to be supported.

"Stay here," Darby urged. "As soon as we get back to the
Comstock Lode I'll tell your father what happened and he'll
send you help."

"I'll be a dead man before you're gone an hour," Alexander
said. "Jasper knows he can't dare allow me to tell my father
about his murderous behavior."

"But you said you didn't have any proof he'd poisoned you
or any others. Nor that he was behind the ambushing."

"He can't afford to take the chance that I'm only saying
that to keep from being . . . eliminated," Alexander said
with a nervous gulp.

"He's right," Dolly said, coming up from behind. "Bert
Jasper will deliver Alexander in a canvas bag lashed over the
back of one of his mules. He'll have a story that no one will be
able to break. We have to take Alexander with us, Darby."

Darby dipped his chin in reluctant agreement. "Let's get
out of here. The second string of Jasper's mules will be here
in a few minutes and they'll take the rest of the five tons back
to his wagons. After that, we're in a race."

"Don't forget the other competitors," Dolly said.

Darby seriously doubted that any of them were still alive,
much less in the race. They said goodbye to Carl Hanson and
his handful of miners. Zack had this parting bit of advice as

Jasper and his second string of mules grew near: "Get yourselves armed to the teeth and don't do nothing but watch
them back-shooters until they finish loading up and pull out."

"Don't worry, that's what we intend to do," Hanson promised. "And Mr. Poole?"

Alexander, sitting atop a camel, looked down. "Yes?"

"If something bad should happen to us, you'll make sure
that the Consolidated Mining Company takes care of our
families, won't you?"

Alexander bit his lower lip. "You have my word, Carl."

"Thanks."

"Let's go!" Bear shouted. "This is still a race!"

He was right. Only heading back to the Comstock, they
were going to be mostly walking instead of riding because the
camels were so burdened with ore. Dolly and Alexander, being the weakest, could take turns riding the speckled dun
camel that was carrying the lightest load of their supplies.
That would help.

Darby grabbed a jaw rope and started retracing their steps
north. "Let's get them moving! That alone ought to keep
their little minds off Mohammed."

With the hounds worrying the Comstock Camels south-
ward, they moved out very briskly. A herd of abandoned burros, perhaps sensing they'd die without Darby's barrels of
water, came streaming along behind. For better than an hour,
Darby could hear Mohammed's lonely, plaintive cries as they
hurried north back across the sandy desert floor. The temperature, even at three or four o'clock in the morning, was still
over a hundred degrees. Darby was not a bit sure that he
would be able to stand tomorrow's torturous midday heat.
When they passed the mule string, Bert Jasper cursed at them
something terrible and it was all that Darby could do to keep
Zack and Bear from opening fire on their enemies.

"We should have shot them bastards down at the mine,"
Bear grumbled. "Not doing so will come to haunt us, mark
my words."

This dire prediction was still fresh in Darby's mind a little later when they came upon what remained of the burro pack train. The burros were standing about braying in confusion as their masters lay in the dirt with cut throats.

"Holy God!" Alexander cried.

"Damn them!" Dolly swore.

Darby came to a stop as the burros, finally catching wind of the camels, scattered out into the desert. "We've got to bury these men."

Bear objected. "That first string of mules has got to be around here somewhere! And Jasper will break his neck getting back to join 'em. They could do it before we finished burying these poor souls."

"Then we'll have our showdown right here," Darby told them. "Perhaps it would be better to get it over now one way or the other."

Not surprisingly, it was Alexander who disagreed. "We'd not stand a chance against so many," he said. "Our only hope is to outrun them."

"We can't do that with our camels staggering under such heavy loads of ore."

"Then let's dump the damned ore!" Alexander cried. "My father would understand!"

Bear and Zack wouldn't hear of it. "The race rules are plain. If we break 'em, we'd never hear the end of it and we wouldn't have won the contract."

"But I helped my father *make* the rules!"

Zack and Bear weren't impressed. They folded their arms across their chests and looked to Darby for help.

"They're right," Darby said to the young man. "The rules are the rules. If we decide to dump the ore and run for our lives, we give up the chance of winning the contract."

"And we won't do that," Bear said.

"No," Zack said, "we won't."

Alexander shook his head with amazement. "You're all crazy! So what if we dump the ore? My father and I will just send wagons down for it this fall when it's cooler."

Darby looked up to see that Emil was awake and was glaring down at them. Darby turned back to Alexander. "It's a matter of principle," he said, knowing that his explanation sounded hollow. "We agreed to do a thing and we're going to do it."

"Even if it costs us our lives?"

"Even if we have to fight," Darby answered.

"Miss Beavers," Alexander cried. "Talk some sense into these people! They must be addled by the sun!"

Dolly shook her head. "They're not addled," she said, "they're just brave men who agreed to do a thing no matter how hard or how great the risk."

"This is insane!"

Darby had heard enough. He handed his camel's rope to Dolly. "We'll see if we can find some shovels," he said. "This ground is far sandier than that which we dug graves in before. It won't take very long to bury these men."

Dolly touched Darby's cheek and said, "I'm sorry about what I said back at the mine. I just didn't realize that you hated Mohammed so much."

"Well," Darby said, "I did. He ruined two good suits with green spit. Furthermore, he was mean-spirited and a big coward."

"Emil loved him."

"Emil needs a woman, not a camel."

Dolly elected not to comment on that. Instead, she said, "How long are you going to keep Emil hogtied?"

"I don't know," Darby admitted. "I'm half afraid he'll find his weapons and use them on me."

"Would you blame the man?"

"I guess not," Darby said, knowing that the Arab felt betrayed. "But I still believe I did what had to be done in order to avoid a slaughter back at Gold Peak. Don't you?"

"Now I do," Dolly said. "I didn't see it at the time. I'm sorry."

"It's all right," Darby said, going off after Bear and Zack to search for shovels.

The burial was accomplished in less than two hours. The

sun, a molten ball of brass, lifted off the tabletop of the earth as the Comstock camels were driven north by the hounds. Much later in the day, Darby heard a weak, distant but quite distinct sound. He came to a halt and his camel whipped its head around and began to squawk. All eleven camels took up the call and it grew louder until Mohammed came flying over a low, sandy hillock, jaw rope trailing and six arrows sticking out of his haunches.

"Holy cow!" Zack shouted. "Look at them arrows stickin' out of his butt!"

Dolly squealed with outrage. "How terrible!"

Darby felt awful and even Bear and Zack shot him disgusted looks as they hurried back to catch the big camel. Because Emil was wiggling like crazy, Darby cut his bonds. The little Arab dropped to the sand and landed on his back before he shot off to catch and doctor Mohammed.

It took another hour for Emil to remove the arrows and smear some kind of grease on Mohammed's backside.

"I'd say from the looks you're getting," Alexander commented, "that you are not very popular right now."

"That," Darby said, "is the height of understatement."

"How is he?" Darby asked the two mountain men just before they resumed their race northward.

Zack said, "The camel or the Arab?"

"Both."

"The camel's goin' to live, judgin' by his bawlin', but his backside's in pretty sorry condition."

Darby nodded. Mohammed had not stopped squawking since his arrival. "And Emil El Babba?"

"We'll cover *your* backside," Zack said.

"Thanks," Darby replied, wondering who wanted to kill him the most, the Arab—or Dolly.

Eighteen

BY MID-MORNING, Darby knew that they were not going to outrun Bert Jasper's outfit back to Silver City. In the first place, it was just too damned hot to hurry across the desert on foot, and in the second place, Mohammed refused to move at anything faster than a turtle's pace. The huge camel hadn't stopped bawling since being pincushioned with arrows.

And if all that wasn't enough, the pack string of burros they'd been forced to adopt were all trailing along behind making a general nuisance of themselves. The little "desert canaries," as they were affectionately dubbed by Nevada prospectors, stayed about a hundred yards behind Mohammed. They brayed, snorted and curled their upper lips to indicate that they detested the strange stench of camel, but they were smart enough to want their share of the caravan's life-giving water. No one had the heart or energy to drive them away. In fact, just before daybreak, Darby had unloaded a water barrel and watered the parched critters.

"I count twenty-seven," Dolly lamented. "How are we going to keep so many alive? We don't have enough water."

"I don't know," Darby confessed. "All we can do is push on and do the best we can."

About noon, Zack made a pronouncement. "Jasper and his outfit will overtake us by tomorrow at the latest. The best thing we can do is to pick a spot and try and ambush 'em."

Bear disagreed. "Ambush 'em on this desert? What are you talkin' about, Zack? There's no place to hide out here 'cept in one of these arroyos."

"Then that's where we ought to hide," Zack said stubbornly. "Some of 'em are plenty deep enough to hide the camels."

"I say we dump the ore," Alexander argued, "and leave Mohammed behind. The healthy camels will move a whole lot faster."

"We aren't leaving poor Mohammed behind," Dolly vowed. "Not unless we leave Emil out here with him."

Darby took another drink of water and watched as the others had their fill. The camels had already been given a full barrel of water this day but it had barely slaked their enormous thirsts. If left to their own desires, each camel was capable of inhaling an entire barrel.

"An ambush," Zack repeated, "is our only hope of evenin' the odds in our favor."

Darby removed his canvas hat and held it up to shield his eyes from the sun as he examined the immensity of this baking desert. Layers of heat waves undulated across his vision. It was so hot Darby felt as if the soles of his feet were on fire.

"Let's get moving," he said at last. "It will be dark in a few more hours and we can travel until midnight."

"If they catch sight of us, we won't be able to ambush 'em," Zack warned ominously.

Without comment, Darby pushed wearily onward. He could hear the others grumbling and arguing in the background along with Mohammed's bawling and an occasional yip from one of the hounds as it snapped at a camel's hocks.

Ignoring his own misery, Darby focused on the image of beautiful Lake Tahoe with its sparkling emerald-green waters. It seemed years since he, Dolly, Bear and Zack had almost drowned in that storm-tossed lake, and the memory of its cool wetness soothed his mind. He vowed to himself that, should they survive this desert, he would return with Miss Beavers to Lake Tahoe and plunge headlong into its icy waters. He would rejoice at his goosebumps and chattering teeth. He would shiver in ecstasy and swim until his bones ached with cold. Later, he would sip brandy and smoke cigars as he worked on his first camel dime novel in the shade of the huge ponderosa pines.

What a scenic mountain paradise that and searing desert hell this!

Much later, the punishing sun finally burned into the gray outline of the distant Sierra Nevada Mountains and the temperature cooled a few blessed degrees. Lost in the vast emptiness of a desert sea that rippled endlessly before him, Darby's mind continued to revel in cool vistas of lush mountain forests, placid blue lakes and gushing mountain streams. Darby picked out the North Star and followed it on and on until he could no longer put one foot down before the other. Sagging to his knees, still clutching the shotgun, he bowed his head and sucked in deep drafts of hot air.

"Darby? Darby!"

He shook his head and looked up into Dolly's moonlit face.

"Darby, we can't walk all the way back to the Comstock Lode in this terrible heat! We *must* dump the ore and ride these camels or we won't make it!"

Zack and Bear joined them and solemnly agreed.

Zack said, "It's another four or five days to the Walker River. We won't make it afoot. We've got to make our stand while we've still got our senses and strength to fight."

Alexander saw things a little differently. "I say we just drop the ore and run for it!"

"Button it up!" Darby exploded.

Alexander recoiled in shock.

Darby regretted his loss of composure. "I regret that outburst," he said a little apologetically, "but you have to realize, Alexander, that your opinions don't amount to doodly squat."

"Mr. Buckingham! I take umbrage at that remark!"

Darby ignored the young man, who was the only one among them who had not taken a turn walking this terrible day. "All right," he said, unable to mount a creditable argument and fearing his own endurance was ebbing fast, "we'll make a stand and fight."

"Good!" Zack exclaimed. He pointed off to the northeast.

"Bear and I studied that long sand dune over yonder. We can get behind it and make a stand right there."

Darby studied the distant ridge of white, moonlit sand. It was at least twenty feet tall, more than high enough to hide them as well as the Comstock camels. "What if Jasper and his men just pass us by and keep going to the Comstock?"

It was obvious that none of them had even considered such a possibility. Alexander said it for all of them when he commented, "Jasper and his men are murderers. They can't afford to let us reach the Comstock Lode. They know that I'll tell my father about the murders Jasper and his men have committed. Proof or no proof, I guarantee that our company will not award a freighting contract to Bert Jasper under any circumstances."

"All right," Darby said. "Then let's make our stand."

It took them an hour to reach and climb over the immense sand dune. Once over the top, Emil hobbled Mohammed and turned him loose. The wounded camel headed right for the nearest patch of sage and the other camels followed. Unfortunately, the burros refused to be lured behind the dune but instead elected to scatter out before it, braying and nibbling at the stunted clumps of sage.

"What are we going to do with them?" Dolly asked.

"Nothing," Darby said.

"But they'll give our hiding place away!"

"So," Darby pointed out, "will our tracks. There has never been the option of surprise. If Jasper chooses to attack us, then so be it."

Darby smoothed Dolly's hair. He had never seen her look so exhausted. "My dear," he said with far more assurance than he really felt, "don't you worry. We'll do all right even if Jasper does choose to attack. As for the present, I suggest we get a little sleep before Jasper's outfit arrives."

Dolly was so tired it was all she could do to nod her head and lie down on the warm sand. She fell asleep almost instantly and Darby fell asleep as well.

They all slept like the dead during what remained of the

night, confident that Sid and Slick would alert them to any approaching danger. Daybreak broke in its usual spectacular fashion, firing the desert vermilion and causing the temperature to soar. The burros, desperate with thirst, came trotting over the dune and were rationed a few precious cupfuls of water. Because of their severe shortage of water, the camels would have to wait.

"Here they come," Bear said, his head poking over the dune they were hiding behind. "Look!"

Darby slithered up the hot dune until he was positioned just below its crown. He removed his wide-brimmed hat and squinted to see the line of ore wagons and struggling mules. Although still several miles distant, it was plain that the heavily laden wagons were having a bad time getting through the sandy stretches that puddled the desert's floor. Men were staggering along beside the wheels, grabbing them and pushing whenever the wagons threatened to become mired.

Bear and Zack inspected their big Hawken rifles. Zack said, "Bert Jasper won't be hard to spot. I say we both drill him first. Maybe the others will just give up."

"Right."

Darby was shocked. "You can't just shoot him from ambush!"

"Why not?" Bear demanded.

"Because!"

"That ain't no answer," Zack growled.

"Then because it's wrong! It's murder!"

"It's *dead* is what it is," Bear said matter-of-factly. "With Jasper dead, we might even get to stay alive long enough to win us that freight contract."

"Uh-oh," Zack muttered. "They're stopping where we angled off the road."

Darby watched with more than a casual interest as Jasper and his men held a hurried council. Even at this distance Darby could see that there was a lively debate under way.

"Come on!" Zack pleaded, sleeving sweat from his brow. "Come and get us, Jasper!"

But Jasper wasn't among the four men who mounted mules and came riding in their direction.

"Damn!" Bear swore.

"No matter," Zack said, ducking back down behind the ridge. "If we let them get close enough, we can get all four. Those mules are in no shape to run."

Darby raised his shotgun and fired both barrels. This caused the herd of burros and the Comstock camels to bolt and, had Mohammed not been lame and hobbled, the entire bunch might have taken off running like the burros, who scattered in fright.

"Dammit!" Zack shouted. "Jasper's scouts are turnin' tail on us!"

Zack and Bear both took aim and fired almost simultaneously. They were, however, hopelessly out of range.

"Well," Alexander said with disgust, "we've just thrown away any chance we had of getting out of this alive. I count fifteen men with that ore train. We're outnumbered three to one."

"Oh, shut up!" Bear snapped. "Last thing any of us want to hear is you whinin' and bitchin'."

Alexander's cheeks flushed with anger. "If, by some miracle, we do get out of this alive, you'll have some apologies to make and you'll make them to me, Mr. Timberly."

"In a pig's eye!"

"Settle down, the both of you," Dolly ordered.

"They're going on!" Bear cried. "Look! They're moving north again!"

Zack swore bitterly despite Alexander's assurances that it no longer mattered who won the race. "Don't you understand! They've robbed and murdered the competition! I promise that our Consolidated Mining Company will never give them the contract."

"So what are we gonna do now, for cryin' in the beer?" Bear asked.

"We go after them," Darby said. "What else?"

"But first we dump the ore," Alexander said. "As the road improves nearing the Comstock, our advantage with camels is lost."

Darby was forced to admit that Alexander was correct. He could see now that there was no choice but to dump their ore and try to overtake Jasper's wagon train. "Agreed. We'll leave the ore behind, take our water, food and a few bales of hay for the burros."

And so, with the sun rising higher and hotter, they rushed back to the camels and informed Emil of their plans. The Arab was delighted. Without the great burden of Gold Peak ore, his camels could move much faster and reach Walker Lake before they really began to suffer from thirst. He was still furious at Darby for confiscating his weapons and making him suffer the indignity of being lashed across the back of Mohammed, but now believed things would get much better.

When they left the sand dune and angled back to the road, the camels seemed to understand the urgency of overtaking the mules and wagons up ahead. Mohammed stopped squawking and the burros fell silent as they hurried along in a steady trot.

Late that afternoon, Darby twisted around on his camel and was about to shout a word of encouragement to Dolly when, suddenly, he realized they were being overtaken by a large band of Paiutes. Several hundred of them at least. He blinked, thinking they might be a mirage, but they weren't. The Paiutes were lithe, dark-skinned warriors and they were carrying bows and quivers of arrows.

"We've got a big problem!" Darby shouted.

Everyone twisted around and when they saw the rapidly closing Indians, Darby felt a spear of panic shoot through them. "Emil, they want Mohammed back! And if they can't have him, they'll put more arrows in his bottom. So I'm asking you, can all these 'beautiful' camels run?"

Emil raised his whip and shouted, "We run, boss!"

And run they did. It was terrifying to ride a galloping

camel. Each rider was whipped back and forth like a rubber ball on the end of a string. Darby grabbed everything. Mohammed, forgetting his arrow wounds, shot out into the lead and the others stretched out their long, skinny necks and went after their leader. Sid and Slick, tongues practically dragging on the sand, yelped with fear and ran even harder when the Paiutes began to howl in anger at being discovered. The burros brayed and their furry little legs churned madly.

Darby did not dare look back. On and on they galloped, much faster than a man could run. The camels squawked and the huge bellows of their lungs worked mightily as they extended the distance between themselves and the howling Paiutes.

At sundown when the Paiutes had dropped far out of sight, Emil drew Mohammed to a walk. For ten minutes, they just let the camels blow.

"What are we going to do now?" Alexander asked, voicing the question that consumed all of their minds. "Jasper is just up ahead of us, and the Paiutes are right behind. We're in an awful fix, Mr. Buckingham."

"That we are," Darby agreed. "My hope is that Jasper has made camp. He won't expect us to attack his far superior force, but that's what we must do. I say we make a wide circle around his camp and hit him just before daybreak from the north where he least expects it."

"Good idea," Zack said, "but aren't you forgetting the Indians?"

"No. If they attack, it will probably also be at dawn and they'll strike Jasper instead of us."

Bear grinned. "Say, I like that!"

"I don't," Alexander said, "but it makes good sense."

"Of course it does," Dolly said, looking at Darby with pride. "Jasper and his murderers will be caught in the vise instead of us."

Darby headed his weary camel off to make a wide loop around where he hoped Jasper's camp would be and all the while he prayed silently that he had not miscalculated. If Jasper had decided not to stop for the night, or if . . .

"Stop it," Darby growled to himself. "Remember those shooting stars? Well, tonight they had just better bring us that long overdue good luck."

Nineteen

DARBY BUCKINGHAM silently raised his shotgun overhead as if to salute the moon. A hundred yards before him, Bert Jasper's camp could easily be seen due to its low, flickering campfire. A mile to the safety of the north waited Dolly, Emil, the hounds, the burros and the camels.

Darby dropped to his knees in the hot sand. His eyes burned from lack of sleep and the salt of his sweat. He was so weary that he had to speak with care lest he create even a trace of confusion in Zack, Bear and Alexander Poole.

"As you all can see," he whispered, adjusting a sixgun jammed into his waistband to a more comfortable position, "their wagons are pulled into a half circle hubbed by the campfire. There are probably some men sleeping in the wagons but most are lying around the fire. So we go in, get the drop on them and when I shout, 'Freeze!' we make sure they are well covered."

Alexander cleared his throat and clutched his own sixgun. "Mr. Buckingham, this isn't one of your famous dime novels. Do you really think they'll all just surrender?"

"I would if I were them," Darby said, reasoning out loud. "You see, the only one among them that will probably be tried for murder is Bert Jasper. The others will only be jailed or chased off the Comstock. That's far better than being gunned down in our crossfire."

"I suppose," Alexander said, not sounding very convinced.

Darby looked to the mountain men. "Are there any more questions?"

"No questions," Bear said. "Only we'd all better understand that Jasper will shoot it out before he surrenders. Could be a few others of the same mind."

"That's quite possible," Darby conceded, "but we will give them the chance to surrender. If they decide otherwise . . ."

Darby did not need to finish the statement. They all realized that, if the shooting started, it was every man for himself. Outnumbered better than three to one, it would be a hard, desperate fight and some of them would not live to watch another spectacular Mojave sunrise.

"Let's go," Darby said, coming to his feet but staying as low as he could as they crept up on the ore wagons.

They filtered through a band of mules too weak and weary to do anything but snort. By moving slowly and whispering soft assurances, Darby and his companions managed to reach Jasper's ore wagons without detection.

Darby motioned for Bear and Zack to circle to his left. He knew that, if the need arose, the two mountain men would fire their Hawken rifles, then draw their Bowie knives. When that happened, blood and sand would mix.

"Alexander, are you ready?" Darby whispered.

"As ready as I'll ever be," Alexander breathed. "Have you ever killed anyone before, Derby Man?"

"Yes," Darby took no pleasure in admitting, "but I hope not to tonight."

"Same here."

Darby eased between the wagons, his eyes skipping from one sleeping figure on the ground to another, hoping to spot the immense outline of Bert Jasper. But the giant wasn't bedded down beside the campfire. Darby eased up on the tongue of the nearest ore wagon and peered inside. He saw nothing and was debating whether or not to search all the wagons for Jasper when one of the men on the ground sat upright and began to babble incoherently. The man's face was terrified in the firelight and it was obvious that he was in the grip of a nightmare because he shouted, "No, Maude, I swear I didn't . . ."

Darby never learned what outrage the man had committed against poor Maude because the confused man leaped to his feet and ran headlong into Bear and Zack.

Zack's Hawken slashed a clean arc and its barrel cracked against the side of the man's skull. He staggered backward, tripped and tumbled into the embers of the dying campfire. The dazed and terrified soul screeched like a panther, then sprang to his feet and vanished into the predawn darkness.

All hell broke loose as Jasper's crew clawed for their weapons. Muzzle flashes winked like fireflies and Darby felt a shot sting wickedly across his shoulder. He heard Alexander's gun banging wildly and when three men jumped up and opened fire, Darby unleashed the twin fury of both shotgun barrels. The three went down like tall corn in a high wind.

Darby dropped his empty shotgun and yanked the Colt revolver from his waistband as he yelled, "Freeze! Everyone freeze!"

Some froze, most lost their nerve and ran, a foolish few chose to fight and die. It all happened so fast and with such violence that the battle lasted mere seconds.

"Are you all right?" Darby shouted, spinning around to where he'd last seen Alexander.

To Darby's shock, Alexander was anything but all right. He was holding a smoking but empty gun at his side as Bert Jasper pressed a Colt to the base of his young neck. Darby realized that Bear and Zack each had a fistful of Bowie knife while he alone held a sixgun.

"Drop it, Buckingham, or I'll blow this dude's brains apart!"

"Darby," Zack pleaded, "if you drop that gun, we're *all* dead men!"

"He's right!" Alexander said bravely. "Just shoot him, Mr. Buckingham. I'm a dead man anyway."

"Don't listen to him," Jasper yelled. "If you drop your gun, Alexander will live and so will the rest of you. All I want is a saddle mule to ride out of here!"

"He's lying!" Bear shouted. "If we all three rush him we . . ."

Jasper jammed the barrel of his Colt even harder against Alexander's neck, driving him to his toes. "Drop that gun or I'll shoot!"

"Kill him, Mr. Buckingham! What are you waiting for? Shoot!"

Darby raised the Colt and took aim but he was a terrible shot and he knew he would either miss or hit young Alexander. Most likely, Alexander would die and so would he before Bear and Zack could use their knives on the giant. On the other hand, Darby was quite sure they were all dead if he dropped his sixgun.

Jasper cocked the hammer of his pistol. "I'm givin' you just five seconds to fish or cut bait, Buckingham. You'll either drop that gun or we're all going to hell on the same ticket."

"Maybe we can come to some better arrangement," Darby blurted, playing for time while desperate possibilities whirled in his mind.

"Such as?"

"I don't know! But you can't take all three of us down. Not by yourself."

Jasper barked a contemptuous laugh. "My boys will soon come back to help me. You killed a few, but a bunch got away. They'll be here in a minute or two. So drop your gun, Buckingham. You've lost."

Alexander suddenly slammed the heel of his boot down on Jasper's bare toes. He not only crushed them, but he ground them under his heel. The giant slashed him across the head with the barrel of his Colt and turned his sixgun on Darby.

Their shots blended. Darby felt a bullet whip-crack past his right ear. He dropped to his knees and kept squeezing the trigger, not bothering to aim because that never helped anyway.

The Derby Man's first two bullets were way wide. But his third bullet struck Jasper in the arm and his fourth smashed through Jasper's ribs and punctured the giant's right lung before it exited his back.

Jasper staggered and his huge frame shivered as he struggled to raise his Colt. Darby held his fire as the giant clasped his wrist and tried to line his sights on Darby but failed.

"Damn you!" Jasper wheezed as he crashed over backward.

A moment later, Darby heard a tremendous roar like a stick of dynamite going off in their midst. He whirled to see Emil El Babba with a huge, roiling cloud of smoke swirling from the flared muzzle of his blunderbuss. One of Jasper's wounded gunfighters who had been about to shoot Darby now collapsed and died.

"Thanks, Emil. Thanks for saving my life."

"Sure, boss."

Somewhere out in the sage, a coyote howled. Then Sid and Slick, followed by Dolly, converged around the bloody campfire. Dolly threw her arms around Darby and hugged and kissed him until he blushed with pleasure.

"What do we do now?" Bear asked. "We've still got Paiutes a'comin'."

Before Darby could form an answer, one of Jasper's deserters barreled into the camp, eyes round with terror. "Don't shoot! There's Indians ready to attack!"

This discovery came as no surprise to Darby and his companions but it sure did to the survivors of Jasper's crew, who rushed back into the camp to surrender rather than be scalped. When the men were all disarmed and under guard, Darby and his friends held a council. Their decision was to reload, stay alert and wait out the coming dawn. If it became obvious that they were going to be overrun by the Paiutes, they would agree to rearm Jasper's men and let them stand and fight.

When dawn finally burned a line across the eastern horizon, it brought heat, light and Indians.

"We're surrounded," Bear said to no one in particular as he revolved full circle.

Darby could see that this was so. The Paiutes had encircled

the entire wagon camp. Off in the distance, a few Paiutes had already butchered a mule and Darby's nostrils twitched at the stench of burning hair and hide. Emil kept his camels very close by the wagons; his saber and his blunderbuss were very much in evidence.

"We can take 'em," Bear said.

"I doubt it," Darby replied.

"We should make peace and give them back that big camel," Alexander said. "Maybe if we did that, they'd be happy and leave us alone."

"It's certainly worth a try," Darby said, turning to Emil. "We need to give them back Mohammed."

"No! They kill and eat!"

"Only if they can't use him to carry their belongings and help make their daily lives easier," Darby argued. "Somehow, we have to make them see how valuable a camel is if one knows how to make it carry a riding or pack saddle."

It made sense. Everyone, even the surviving members of Jasper's band of cutthroats, turned hopefully to the Arab.

"Come on," Darby pleaded. "We've got to work something out or we're all going to die. If they don't attack and kill us right away, they'll wait us out until our water barrels are dry and we are raving mad with thirst."

After a difficult moment, Emil finally nodded his head.

"Good!" Darby cried, not at all sure what he would have done had the Arab chosen to object. "Emil, get Mohammed and we'll see if we can bargain him for our lives."

Darby hugged Dolly, then gave her to Bear for safekeeping. "If we fail, give these hostages their weapons. Maybe you can hold off a charge."

"Maybe," Bear replied, but it was clear he had his doubts.

Just before going out to face the warring Paiutes, Darby glanced sideways at the little Arab and saw that Emil El Babba's face was chiseled stone. His hand gripped the hilt of his long, curved saber and he gave the strong impression of a man heading for the gallows.

"Emil," Darby said as they left camp, "don't you dare get

us killed before I have a chance to talk our way out of this
mess."

A fatalistic grin tugged at both corners of the Arab's mouth.
He gripped his saber until his knuckles whitened and looked
up toward the sky. Darby shivered because he knew the Arab
was looking toward eternity as he marched forward, leading
the limping camel.

"This is it," Darby muttered to himself, his mouth so dry
he could not keep his sandpaper tongue from sticking to the
roof of his wooden mouth. "What a lousy way to die."

By the time they reached the Indians, Waa-so-ah was angrily shouting and pointing at Mohammed. The camel spat at
him but was so dry-mouthed he couldn't muster much more
than a thin green spray. Oh-tah the wood gatherer was smil-
ing but the other Indians wore very serious expressions.
When one of them, a bandy-legged man with silver hair and a
fine wooden bow, began to speak, the others fell silent. Darby
listened and nodded his head as if he understood what the
Paiute chief was saying.

The chief's words finally assumed meaning when, after angrily shaking his bow at Mohammed, the old man pointed to
his own backside. It bore a pair of livid purple welts as thick as
garter snakes. The wrinkled old chief again pointed his bow at
Mohammed, who squawked a pathetic defense.

Now Darby understood a little of what was going on. This
outraged chief had claimed Mohammed as his own and the
camel had bitten him most severely on the buttocks. Mohammed, somewhere in the dim recesses of his self-absorbed little
mind, must have realized he'd made a fatal mistake and he'd
broken away and ran from the Indians, taking several arrows
in his own backside.

Now, in a dramatic fashion, the chief drew his knife and
made a slashing motion across his gullet. He then pointed at
Mohammed and his meaning was ominous and clear.

Emil shook his head vigorously. The chief grew even an-
grier, so Emil drew his sword and hurled himself at the chief.
Darby threw out his leg and the Arab crashed to the ground,

spitting sand and screaming imprecations. Darby landed on
Emil's back and tore the sword from his grasp. When the
Arab kept struggling, Darby cocked his fist back and drove it
to the side of Emil's head hard enough to knock him out cold.

The chief's eyes widened with surprise. He studied the unconscious Arab, then Darby, then turned to Waa-so-ah. The
chief and his medicine man began to talk very rapidly. They
talked so long that Emil began to rouse himself from the
measured blow that Darby had delivered.

Emil tried to come to his feet but Darby would not remove
his knee from the Arab's spine.

"Let me up so that I can die like a man!" Emil cried.

"I'd rather we all lived," Darby said, trying hard to catch
the drift of the Paiute conversation.

"I won't let them slit Mohammed's beautiful throat!"

"He deserves that and more," Darby said without a hint of
sympathy. "But I think the chief has decided that Mohammed
can live—provided his people can have *all* our camels."

Emil's face was caked with sand and his eyes were red and a
little crazed. "What!"

"That's the way I'm reading their talk."

"Never!"

"And they want one more thing."

Emil stopped struggling. "What?"

"You."

"What!"

"That's right. I think they are impressed by your courage
and realize that the Comstock camels are utterly worthless
without America's finest camel man."

"This is what they say?"

"I'm sure of it."

"Get off me, boss."

"If I do, you swear you won't go crazy on me again?"

"Emil El Babba promise."

Darby let the Arab up and even returned his saber. Emil
began to speak to the Paiutes in what Darby imagined was

Arabic. He talked loud and with a great deal of animation. He even smiled and laughed.

Very quickly, the chief was grinning and laughing too and so were the other Paiutes.

After a bewildering half hour of this extraordinary non-sense, Emil turned to Darby and announced, "I'm taking my beautiful camels, boss. I am going away with these beautiful peoples."

Darby blinked, then quickly recovered. "Are you sure?"

"Yes, boss."

"Then of course we'll come and find you . . . when the weather cools," Darby added quickly.

But Emil didn't hear him. "These people will treat me and the camels with respect. No other animals do they have, for this desert would kill all but camels. I will be someone very important with these peoples."

"I suppose so, but . . ."

"And they will have women too," Emil said a little dream-ily. "As a respected man, they will allow me to take a wife."

"That's fine, Emil, but . . ."

"I could never take beautiful camels back across the ocean. So this is good for me. Good for beautiful camels."

Bear, Zack and Dolly joined them and Darby quickly ex-plained the situation.

"Hell," Bear growled, "let him go."

"Yeah," Zack agreed.

"I think it's a wonderful idea," Dolly said, her eyes misty with emotion.

Darby turned back to Emil and they shook hands. He watched as the Arab forced Mohammed to his knees, then he helped the Paiute chief mount the camel. When the old man shot up in the sky, he yelped and grabbed for hair and leather, laughing like a startled child.

All the Paiutes laughed too and so did Dolly. Emil joined the Paiute warriors as he led Mohammed and the other eleven camels south until they drowned in the desert's watery mi-rage.

Bear kicked sand and rumbled, "Even without camels, we've still got the five tons of ore, the wagons and the mules to pull everything on to Silver City."

"I like 'em a lot better'n camels anyway," Zack groused. "Good riddance!"

But Dolly came over to Darby's side, sniffling and blinking back tears. "Will Emil El Babba at last be happy among those Paiutes?"

"He will," Darby said convincingly. "Happier than he's ever been in the American West. He'll take a wife and raise camels and children. He'll be very, very happy."

Dolly hugged Darby as tears coursed down her apple cheeks. Darby grinned because he knew Miss Dolly Beavers was crying for joy.

Author's Note

IN 1855, then Secretary of War Jefferson Davis convinced a skeptical United States Congress that it ought to import camels for the purpose of determining if they were suitable to supply army outposts in the great American Southwest. About seventy-five of the beasts were eventually assembled at Camp Verde, near Bandera Pass, Texas. They soon made their way to the deserts of Arizona, Nevada and California. The army camels had many qualities suitable to the harsh American deserts—they seemed impervious to intense heat and poisonous rattlesnake bites, could subsist on sagebrush, thorns and thistles, and traveled for days without water. Furthermore, they could carry staggering loads, sometimes as much as a thousand pounds.

Unfortunately, no one reckoned with their extremely nasty temperaments. Horses, mules and oxen would stampede at the sight or smell of a camel. The Army's enlisted men, spat upon, kicked and bitten by the beasts, came to hate camels with an enduring passion.

The Comstock Camels is the fruit of this author's own recollections of watching the mayhem of the Virginia City Camel Races with great amusement and sympathy for both the camel riders and handlers. The camel experiment was eventually deemed a failure despite its occasional successes. After passing through many hands over several decades, the surviving camels were finally abandoned in the vast Southwestern deserts, where they lived free for many, many years. Eventually, they disappeared into history, just like their once proud Arab handlers, fellows like my fiery Emil El Babba.

GARY MCCARTHY
Ojai, California